gatekeepers

BOOKS BY THIS AUTHOR

Comes a Horseman

Germ

Deadfall

Deadlock

DREAMHOUSE KINGS SERIES

1 *House of Dark Shadows*

2 *Watcher in the Woods*

3 *Gatekeepers*

4 *Timescape*

5 *Whirlwind* – Available January 2010

Gatekeepers

BOOK THREE OF
DREAMHOUSE KINGS

ROBERT LIPARULO

THOMAS NELSON
Since 1798

NASHVILLE DALLAS MEXICO CITY RIO DE JANEIRO BEIJING

Published in Nashville, Tennessee, by Thomas Nelson. Thomas Nelson is a registered trademark of Thomas Nelson, Inc.

Page design by Mandi Cofer
Map design by Doug Cordes

Thomas Nelson, Inc., titles may be purchased in bulk for educational, business, fund-raising, or sales promotional use. For information, please e-mail SpecialMarkets@ThomasNelson.com.

Publisher's Note: This novel is a work of fiction. Names, characters, places, and incidents are either products of the author's imagination or used fictitiously. All characters are fictional, and any similarity to people living or dead is purely coincidental.

ISBN 978-1-59554-729-3 (trade paper)

Library of Congress Cataloging-in-Publication Data

Liparulo, Robert.
Gatekeepers / Robert Liparulo.
p. cm. — (Dreamhouse Kings ; bk. 3)
Summary: With their mother still missing after going through a Civil War time portal in their spooky house, and their father in jail under a false accusation, Xander, David, and their younger sister continue to try to bring their mother back, now with the help of an old relative who has turned up unexpectedly.
ISBN 978-1-59554-498-8 (hardcover)
[1. Time travel—Fiction. 2. Dwellings—Fiction. 3. Brothers and sisters—Fiction. 4. Supernatural—Fiction.] I. Title.
PZ7.L6636Gat 2009
[Fic]—dc22

2008042007

Printed in the United States of America
HB 06.06.2018

To my daughter Melanie

You may have outgrown my lap,
but never my heart.

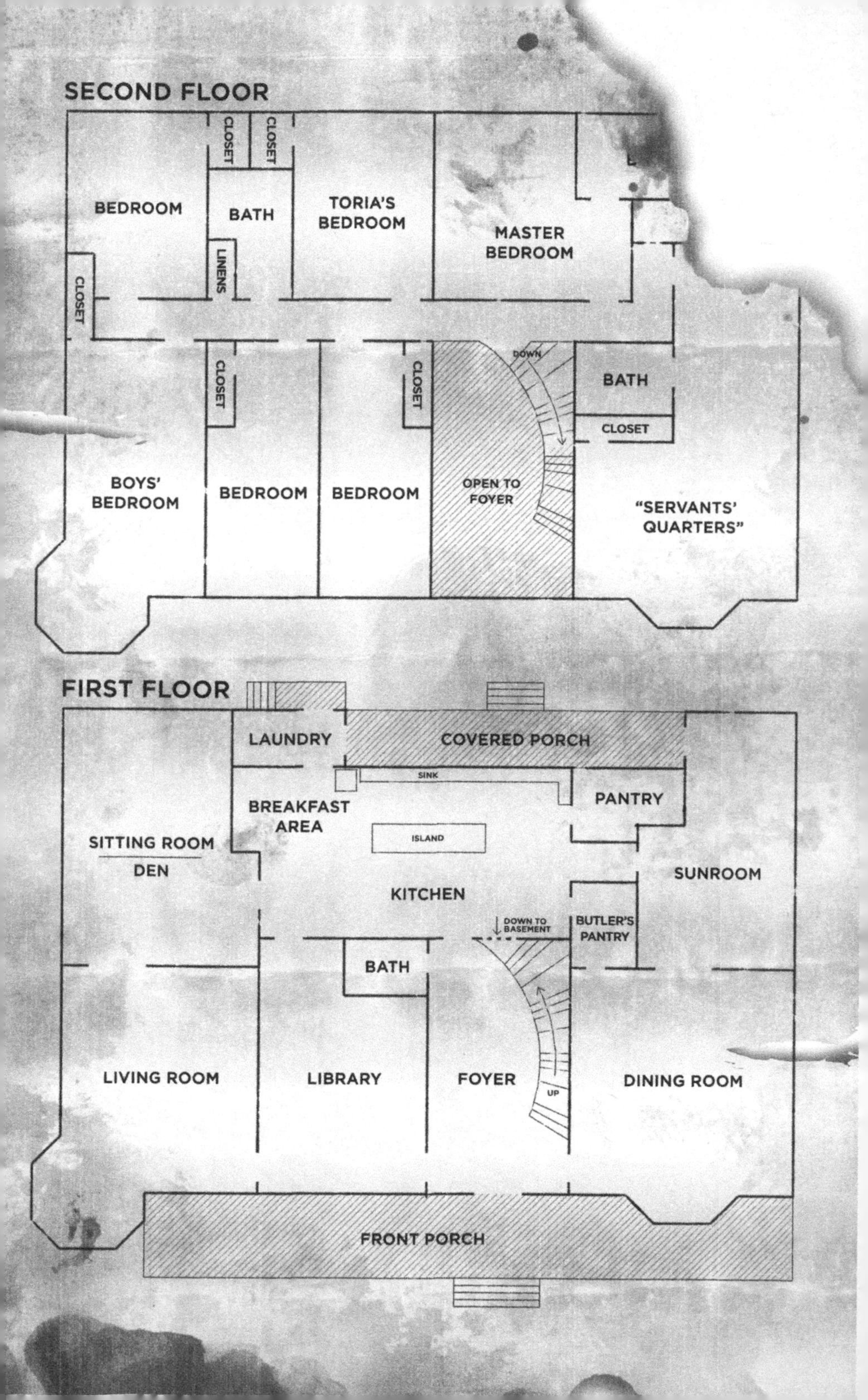
SECOND FLOOR
BEDROOM
CLOSET
CLOSET
BATH
LINENS
TORIA'S BEDROOM
MASTER BEDROOM
CLOSET
CLOSET
CLOSET
DOWN
BATH
CLOSET
BOYS' BEDROOM
BEDROOM
BEDROOM
OPEN TO FOYER
"SERVANTS' QUARTERS"
FIRST FLOOR
LAUNDRY
COVERED PORCH
SINK
PANTRY
BREAKFAST AREA
ISLAND
SITTING ROOM
DEN
SUNROOM
KITCHEN
DOWN TO BASEMENT
BUTLER'S PANTRY
BATH
LIVING ROOM
LIBRARY
FOYER
UP
DINING ROOM
FRONT PORCH

READ *HOUSE OF DARK SHADOWS* AND *WATCHER IN THE WOODS* BEFORE CONTINUING!

"Who are you really, wanderer?"
and the answer you have to give
no matter how dark and cold
the world around you is:
"Maybe I'm a King."

—WILLIAM STAFFORD, *A STORY THAT COULD BE TRUE*

O, call back yesterday, bid time return.

—WILLIAM SHAKESPEARE, *KING RICHARD II*

CHAPTER

one

TUESDAY, 6:58 P.M.
PINEDALE, CALIFORNIA

Xander's words struck David's heart like a musket ball.

He reeled back, then grabbed the collar of his brother's filthy Confederate coat. His eyes stung, whether from the tears squeezing around them or the sand whipping through the room, he didn't know. He pulled his face to within inches of Xander's.

"You . . . you *found* her?" he said. "Xander, you found *Mom?*"

He looked over Xander's shoulder to the portal door, which had slammed shut as soon as Xander stumbled through. The two boys knelt in the center of the antechamber. Wind billowed their hair. It whooshed in under the door, pulling back what belonged to the Civil War world from which Xander had just stepped. The smell of smoke and gunpowder was so strong, David could taste it.

He shook Xander. "Where is she? Why didn't you bring her?"

His heart was going crazy, like a ferret racing around inside his chest, more frantic than ever. Twelve-year-olds didn't have heart attacks, did they?

Xander leaned back and sat on his heels. His bottom lip trembled, and his chest rose and fell as he tried to catch his breath. The wind plucked a leaf from his hair, whirled it through the air, then sucked it under the door.

"Xander!" David said. "Where's Mom?"

Xander lowered his head. "I couldn't . . ." he said. "I couldn't get her. You gotta go over, Dae. You gotta bring her back!"

"Me?" A heavy weight pushed on David's chest, smashing the ferret between sternum and spine. He rose, leaped for the door, and tugged on the locked handle.

He wore a gray hat ("It's a *kepi,*" Dad would tell him) and jacket, like Xander's blue ones. They had discovered that it took wearing or holding three items from the antechamber to unlock the portal door. He needed one more.

"Xander, you said you found her!"

Xander shook his head. "I think I saw her going into a tent, but it was at the other end of the camp. I couldn't get to her."

David's mouth dropped open. "That's not *finding* her! I thought I saw her, too, the other day in the World War II world—"

"Dae, listen." Xander pushed himself up and gripped David's shoulders. "She saw the message we left. She saw Bob."

Bob was the cartoon face and family mascot since Dad was a kid, drawn on notes and birthday cards. When David and Xander had been in Ulysses S. Grant's Union camp the night before, Xander had drawn it on a tent. It was their way of letting Mom know they were looking for her.

"She wrote back!" Xander said. "David, she's *there!*"

"But . . ." David didn't know if he wanted to scream or cry or punch his brother. "Why didn't you go get her?"

"Something was happening on the battlefield. They were rounding up all the soldiers and herding us toward the front line. I tried to get to her, but they kept grabbing me, pushing me out of camp. When I broke away"—Xander's face became hard—"they called me a deserter. That quick, I was a deserter. One of them *shot* at me! I barely got back to the portal." He shook his head. "You gotta go! Now! Before she's gone, or the portal changes, or something happens to her."

Yes . . . no! David's stomach hurt. His brain was throbbing against his skull. His broken arm started to ache again, and he rubbed the cast. "Xander, I can't. They almost killed me yesterday."

"That's because you were a gray-coat." Xander began taking off his blue jacket. "Wear this one."

"Why can't *you*? Just tell them—"

"I'll never make it," Xander said. "They'll throw me in the stockade for deserting—if they don't shoot me first."

"They'll do the same to me." David hated how whiney his words came out.

"You're just a kid. They'll see that."

"I'm twelve, Xander. Only three years younger than you."

"That's the difference between fighting and not, Dae." He held the jacket open. "I know it was really scary before, but this time you'll be on the right side."

David looked around the small room. He said, "Where's the rifle you took when you went over? The Harper's Ferry musket?"

His brother gazed at his empty hand. He scanned the floor. "I must have dropped it when I fell. I was just trying to stay alive. I didn't notice." He shook the jacket. "Come on."

David shrugged out of the gray coat he was wearing. He tossed it onto the bench and reluctantly slipped into the one Xander held. He pulled the left side over his cast.

Xander buttoned it for him. He said, "The tent I saw her

go into was near the back of the camp, on the other side from where I drew Bob." He lifted the empty sleeve and let it flop down. He smiled. "Looks like you lost your arm in battle."

"See? They'll think I *can* fight, that I *have* fought."

"I was just kidding." He took the gray kepi off David's head and replaced it with the blue one. Then he turned to the bench and hooks, looking for another item.

"Xander, listen," David said. "You don't know what's been happening here. There are two cops downstairs."

Xander froze in his reach for a canteen. "What?" His head pivoted toward the door opposite the portal, as though he could see through it into the hallway beyond, down the stairs, around the corner, and into the foyer. Or like he expected the cops to burst through. "What are they doing here?"

"They're trying to get us out of the house. Taksidian's with them." Just thinking of the creepy guy who was responsible for his broken arm frightened David—but not as much as the thought of getting hauled away when they were so close to rescuing Mom. "Gimme that," he said, waggling his fingers at the canteen.

Xander snatched it off the hook and looped the strap over David's head. "Where's Dad?"

"They put him in handcuffs. He told me to come get you."

"Handcuffs!"

"And one more thing," David said. He closed his eyes, feeling as though the jacket had just gained twenty pounds. "Clayton, that kid who wanted to pound me at school? He came through the portal from the school locker to the linen closet." He opened one eye to see his brother's shocked expression.

"How *long* was I gone?" Xander said. "Where is he now?"

"I pushed him back in. He returned to the school, but he might come back."

"Great." Xander glanced over his shoulder at the hallway door again, then back at David. "Anything else I should know?"

David shook his head. "I guess if I die, I won't have to go to school tomorrow." He smiled weakly.

The school year—seventh grade for David, tenth for Xander—had started just yesterday: two days of classes. Mom had been kidnapped the day before that. David couldn't believe they'd even gone to school under the circumstances, but Dad, who was the new principal, had insisted they keep up normal appearances so they wouldn't attract suspicion.

Lot of good it did, David thought, thinking of the cops downstairs.

"I don't know," Xander said. "Dad would probably figure out a way to get your body there."

David's expression remained grim.

"You'll be fine."

"Don't get taken away," David told his brother. "Don't leave with me over there. Don't leave me alone in this house when I come back. Don't—"

Xander held up his hand to stop him. "I won't leave," he said. "I'll go see what's happening downstairs, but I won't leave. No way, no how. Okay? Besides—" He smiled, but David saw how hard it was for him to do it. "You'll have Mom with you when you come back. Right?"

It was David's turn to smile, and he found it wasn't so hard to do. "Yeah." He turned, took a deep breath, and opened the portal door.

CHAPTER

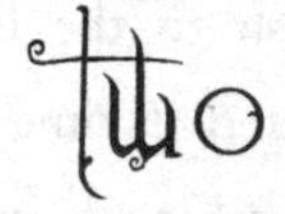

TUESDAY, 7:05 P.M.

David squinted against the bright daylight coming through the portal. A warm breeze touched his face. The odor of gunpowder wafted into his nostrils. It reminded him of his time on the battlefield, and he felt sick again.

"Go," Xander said behind him.

"I am." He stepped through, stumbled, and fell into a bush. He rolled out of it and cracked his cast into a tree. He pulled air through his clenched teeth. Before the portal faded and broke apart like a defective DVD image, he caught a glimpse of Xander looking through it.

David scrambled up to get his bearings and immediately saw the rows of tents across a narrow meadow. Soldiers streamed toward the far hills, beyond which he knew a battle raged. Gun and cannon fire rang out in the distance. His hope for a deserted camp left him as he spotted more soldiers talking in clusters and others moving from one tent to another.

It wasn't the mad dash to the front line Xander had described, and he wondered if time here had skipped one direction or another, like a hiccup, in the five minutes since his brother had left. They hadn't thought of that. Maybe Xander *could* have returned safely. David looked for the portal, any sign of it, but it was gone.

The first time any of them had gone through a portal, Dad had ended up rescuing Xander from a gladiator. He said the items from the antechamber had tugged him toward the portal home. David and Xander had followed the same tugging to get out of the Civil War world the night before. It was as though the items wanted to go home too, and they knew the way. Now, however, the jacket, kepi, and canteen were exerting no unnatural pull. It was like they knew it wasn't time to return.

Get moving, David told himself, but his feet wouldn't obey.

Even this far away from the battle, smoke drifted over him. *Don't get sick, not now, not with Mom waiting.*

Mom. The thought of her unglued his feet. He lurched forward and out of the woods. Approaching the backs of the tents, he tried to remember which one Xander had written on. Had it been two tents from the front or ten? He had no clue. He walked behind the big wedge-shaped structures, peering between them, hoping to spot something he recognized. And he did, but not what he had expected: the Harper's Ferry rifle Xander had dropped. He must be close to where Xander had drawn Bob and, later, where he'd seen Mom.

David picked up the rifle and walked to the front of the tents, coming out in the camp's center aisle. He turned in a circle, but he didn't see the cartoon face. He headed toward the rear of the camp. Four tents along, he saw it—and his heart leapt into his throat. Just as Xander had said, words were scrawled in block letters beside the goofy face: IS THAT YOU? I'M HERE! I'M

Mom! It had to be! Who else knew the face? Who else would write those words?

But what else had she wanted to write? She had obviously been interrupted: "I'M . . . " I'm what? I'm safe? I'm hurt? I'm at this place or that?

Mom, where are you?

Which tent had Xander seen her enter? He remembered it was on the other side of the aisle. Could she still be there? It struck David that he could be in the camp *before* the events

Xander had witnessed—time was *that* weird with the portals; she might not have even entered the tent yet.

Don't start freaking out now, he told himself. *I can do this: find Mom!*

He looked up the aisle one direction, then down the other. Only men—most of them in blue soldier uniforms, some in the bloodied, once-white smocks of surgeons. A soldier was pounding the butt of his rifle against a rock, a blackened metal pot beside him. David had learned that coffee was cherished in Civil War encampments; this was how they ground the beans. Another man sat on the ground, writing on a piece of paper on his thigh. Two men sat on a log, cleaning their rifles. He wanted to ask whether any of them had seen her. He wanted to call out for her. But did he really want to attract attention to himself?

He started for the tents across the aisle, then thought of something. If she knew they were looking for her there, wouldn't she stay close if she could? He returned to the tent bearing Bob's face and threw back the flap. A soldier sat at the edge of a cot, pulling on his boots. Another lay on a different cot, a rag over his face.

The soldier with the boots looked up. "What do you want, boy?"

David backed away, letting the flap fall into place. He moved toward the next tent. He'd check a few on this side, then cross to the other.

"Hey!" It was a man's deep voice. "You, boy!"

David spun to see the bearded officer who had spoken to him yesterday—General Grant. He was limping now. David couldn't remember if he had limped the day before.

As he drew close, the general expertly flipped up the cover of his gun holster with his thumb. He laid his hand on the handle of his pistol and said, "Drop the rifle, son."

"But—" The word squeaked out of David's tight throat.

General Grant's eyes narrowed. "If I pull this pistol on you, boy, I'll use it. Now drop it."

David forced his fingers to open. The gun hit the trampled earth with a thud. He said, "Sir, I—"

"I know you," Grant said. "Last time I saw you, you wore Confederate gray. Now you're wearing blue and carrying a rifle. Where's the soldier who was escorting you to the stockades?"

He meant Xander. They had pretended to be soldier and prisoner to get David off the front lines without getting shot. "I . . . sir . . . he . . ."

The general shook his head. "We better not find him dead, boy." He turned and raised his hand to a passing soldier. "Corporal!"

David dropped to the ground and started to scramble under the edge of the tent. He heard General Grant say, "Oh, no, you don't!" and felt the man grab his heel.

He yanked his foot out of his sneaker, rose, and ran through the tent, jumping over cots and the men sleeping on them. He slid under the tent's back wall as though he were sliding into home plate. His head snagged on the canvas wall. He ducked, and the cloth wall snapped away.

Behind him the general was yelling, "Escaped Rebel!"

David pictured the man pushing through the tent flaps, pistol in hand. He expected to hear a shot any second. Instead, a commotion arose from within the tent: the clamor of soldiers jumping to their feet, going for their weapons, calling out for someone to tell them what was going on.

"Get down, men!" General Grant bellowed. "Out of my way!"

David got his feet under him and ran for the trees. Kicking through the meadow's tall grass, gritting his teeth against the pain of his cast banging against his ribs, he got the feeling of déjà vu: hadn't he run for his life through this very field before?

Yeah, last night!

Only then Xander had been with him. And he'd had both sneakers. Now he was loping along, one shoe on and one shoe off.

He was almost in the woods when the first shot rang out. Though he had been expecting it, the *crack!* of the weapon startled him. His feet did a little dance, and he tumbled over himself. Up again in no time, he plunged into the shadows of the trees. Behind him, another rifle shot cracked. He pushed deeper into the woods, then rammed his shoulder into the trunk of a big oak. He rolled around to the tree's far side and stopped. His breathing came in ragged gulps.

David hadn't bothered to grab the rifle when he'd bolted away from General Grant. He raised his hand to his head and confirmed what he expected: he'd also lost his kepi. But he still wore the blue jacket, which was now applying a pressure like gravity on his body—only in a *sideways* direction, not downward. If the strength of the tug was any indication, the portal was close. He noticed the canteen. It was lifting up on its strap, vibrating slightly, pointing in the same direction the tug indicated.

He craned his neck to peer past the tree. In the field behind the tents, soldiers were gathering around General Grant. The great man himself was pointing toward the woods, pushing at the soldiers and saying, "Get moving! Go!"

Me too, David thought. *I gotta get out of here.*

He pushed off the tree and ran. The canteen strap rotated on his neck until it floated a few inches off his stomach, directly in front of him. It acted like a compass needle, guiding him toward the portal . . . he hoped.

Behind him a voice yelled, "There!"

Someone fired. The musket ball tore past him, ripping through leaves, snapping branches.

David veered left. For a few steps he ignored the jacket's pull and the canteen's shift to his side. Then he turned back, farther than the canteen's bearing. It swung to his other side.

He zigzagged this way, following the tug of antechamber items, but trying to be a difficult target.

Another shot rang out. Bark exploded from a nearby tree.

A hand grabbed the back of his jacket. He yelled and threw his weight into his forward motion. The canteen hit his chest, slid up and over his shoulder. Its strap tightened around the front of his neck. Nobody had grabbed him, he realized—it was the coat, tugging at him to reverse; he had passed the portal. He skidded to a stop, turned, and ran the other way. The canteen shifted sideways. The jacket urged him to plunge into a thicket of heavy bushes. He stopped, trying to understand.

The corner of his eye caught movement toward the encampment. He turned to see a soldier twenty yards away, taking aim. He stumbled back and tumbled into the bushes. The rifle cracked.

CHAPTER three

The musket ball sailed right over him. David hit the ground hard, flat on his back in a tangle of twigs and leaves. The air whooshed out of his lungs. He tried pulling it back in, but it wouldn't come.

Gotta move! Get up! Go!

Gasping for breath, he scrambled to stand. Not easy with only one good arm and the weight of the cast on the other one. He fell back again. His head smacked the ground—a rock, it was so hard. He realized the light around him was not from the sun. His eyes focused on a lamp mounted to a ceiling.

The antechamber. He was home.

Something struck his leg, a hard kick to it. "Xander?"

But it was the door, closing, dragging his legs with it. He remembered the baseball bat that had broken in two between the door edge and the frame when Mom had been taken. He pulled his legs up quickly, and the door slammed.

He rolled over and pushed himself up on one arm. Foliage fell off him.

"Xander?" he said again, wheezing out the word.

The room was empty. He lowered himself back down, resting his face against the wood planks. He put most of his weight onto the right side of his body, feeling his broken arm throb between his chest and the floor. He closed his eyes and breathed.

Wind hissed into the room, causing the twigs and leaves to flutter, then fly into the air. He watched them zip into the crack under the door. The largest twigs got stuck, and leaves piled up behind them. The twigs cracked and splintered. As they did, they disappeared, along with the leaves, all of it heading back where it had come from—heading back to *when* it had come from.

David stood and stared at the portal door. He didn't expect it to open. He didn't expect anything. His eyes simply needed a place to rest while he came out of a mild daze, as if awaking from a deep sleep. Having brushed that close to death, his emotions should have been raging. Instead, he felt numb. It was as though his mind had said *Enough already!* and flipped a switch. He was thankful for the break.

Slowly, he began to move again. He pulled the canteen's strap over his head and set it on the bench. He dropped his shoulder, allowing the jacket to slide off, and slipped his good arm out of the sleeve. He opened the door and walked into the hallway. He hoped Xander, Dad, and Toria, his nine-year-old sister, had fared better at getting rid of the cops than he had at rescuing Mom.

But when he emerged from the secret doorway on the second floor, he found Xander and Toria hiding in the short hall, peering around the corner toward the grand staircase. Voices drifted up from the foyer.

"I told you," Dad was saying, "you can't search my house. Your warrant or whatever this is limits you to *serving* eviction papers, not *enforcing* them."

"We're not evicting you, sir," a voice said. "We're taking you in for assaulting a police officer."

"Assault? I didn't touch you until you bumped into my hand, trying to come into my house without my permission or the authority to do so. Wait, wait, wait . . . my kids are in the house. You can't take me. It will leave them alone."

"Then call them down," another voice said. "We'll take them with us."

"Kids, stay where you are!" Dad called.

Xander held up his hand and gave David a quiet, "Shhh." Then he looked past David, hope and worry on his face. "Where is she?" he whispered. "Tell me you found her, Dae."

David shook his head. "General Grant recognized me. I had to run, like you did. I didn't even get to the tent you told me about. But, Xander . . ." He gripped his brother's arm. "I saw the message she left."

Love for his mother and disappointment at not finding her welled up from his chest. It dried his mouth and wetted his eyes. So, the emotional numbness had been only temporary, he thought. It was like getting punched in the arm so hard you couldn't feel it for a while.

Xander's sadness showed in his eyes, but he nodded and smiled. *Trying to be the big brother, the brave one,* David thought.

Toria whispered, "Who are you talking about? Mom? What message?"

"I'll tell you later," Xander said. "Now *shhh.*" He looked at David and nodded his head toward the voices. "They've been going at it like that for a while. Dad read the court papers, something about the house being unfit to live in."

"I agree," David said.

Xander scowled at him. "They weren't supposed to get us out of the house, just serve the papers."

"So why don't they just go away, then?"

"Dad asked how much Taksidian paid them to get us out of the house, and that *really* ticked them off. Now they want to take him to jail."

Taksidian's deep voice rolled like thunder up the stairs. "Officers," he said, "Mr. King is correct. You can't take him and leave the children here alone."

Why would Taksidian be pleading their case?

But that wasn't what the man had in mind. The next thing he said was, "Why don't I go get them for you?"

Toria took a step back. Her hand clasped David's.

"Hey," Dad said loudly. "He can't—"

"Sir!" a cop said. "We're handling this. Bill, take Mr. King out to the car."

"No! You can't do this!" Dad yelled.

There was a lot of banging going on down there. David imagined his dad, hands cuffed behind him, getting pulled backward out the door while he kicked out at the cops, at Taksidian. His heels would be striking the floor, hitting the door frame.

Xander started around the corner. David pulled his hand out of Toria's and reached for him. His fingers brushed his brother's shirt, then got a grip on his waistband.

Jerked to a stop, Xander snapped his head around. He was what Mom would have called fightin' mad.

David shook his head. "You'll just make it worse."

"They're taking Dad."

"But you heard him. He wants us to stay here. They'll just take you too. Then where will we be?"

Xander looked from David to Toria. Something in her expression softened his. He flipped a stray strand of hair off her face with his finger and said, "It'll be okay, Toria. Don't worry."

She lowered her head. "First Mom, now Dad."

Below, Taksidian said, "Just give me five minutes."

"Can't let you do that, Mr. Taksidian," the remaining cop said. "It's not your house, sir."

David expected the man to say *Not yet* . . . but what he did say was worse.

"But, Officer Benson," Taksidian said, "there's no place they can hide where I can't find them."

Xander looked over his shoulder at David, his eyes wide.

Outside, Dad was still yelling. David heard their names, but the words were being snatched away by the breeze and the trees and the distance as the cop pulled their father away from the house.

Taksidian wasn't finished. He said, "In the interest of the children's welfare, officer, I can make it worth your while."

"Step outside, sir," Officer Benson said.

David thought the cop sounded angry. Maybe after Dad's accusation of the cops taking money to help Taksidian, this new attempt at a bribe had—finally—grated on the cop's sense of duty.

Slow footsteps echoed downstairs, moving from the foyer to the hollow-sounding planks of the front porch.

"Alexander King, David King, Victoria King," the cop hollered, obviously reading their names. "Last chance to come now." He waited. "We'll return with a court order to remove you by force, if necessary. It's for your own safety."

Silence. Then: "We'll send a car back to wait outside tonight. If you change your minds, go out to the officers. They'll take care of you."

His footsteps took him to the porch. The door closed.

CHAPTER four

TUESDAY, 7:33 P.M.

"Now what?" David said.

Above them, something creaked. Their eyes lifted to the ceiling.

"I'm scared," Toria said.

"Just the house settling," Xander said.

His eyes found David's: Xander didn't believe it, and neither did David.

"What if they do come back to take us out by force?"

David said. "They might board the house up or change the locks."

"I think that'll take some time." Xander licked his lips. "Probably easier now that they arrested Dad. But they can't do anything tonight, no way. I'm more worried about—" He stopped, his eyes dropping to Toria.

"What?" she said. "What are you more worried about?"

"Nothing." He peered around the corner, then walked into the second floor's main hallway and to the top of the stairs.

Toria and David followed him. The foyer was empty, the door was closed.

David thought about how wind always blew into the antechamber after they'd returned from one of the worlds. It pulled everything that belonged to that world back through the door. Something like that had just happened in the foyer. The cops and Taksidian had blown in and taken Dad. But Dad belonged *here*. It wasn't right that they could just take him. The house felt emptier without him—not just one person emptier, but like it had been abandoned for centuries, an ancient tomb.

David felt Toria's hand grab his again. He saw that she also clasped Xander's hand. She looked up at him. "Can you guys sleep in my room tonight? Please?"

David nodded.

Xander said, "Good idea. David, let's go get our stuff. Toria, go clear your floor to make room for us."

They walked hand in hand to Toria's door and released her into her room. Then the boys approached the chair that David had jammed under the linen closet door handle to keep Clayton from coming back through. It was a solid piece of furniture, with spindles that rose from the rear of the seat and ended in a heavy top rail.

David leaned his ear to the door. "I don't hear anything," he whispered.

"How long ago did you send him back?"

"Right before I ran to find you," David said.

"So, what, a half hour?" Xander said. "If he was going to come back tonight, he'd have done it already. He must have gone back to the locker and left. Maybe he'll wake up tomorrow thinking it was a dream."

"Fat chance." David reached for the chair, but Xander stopped him.

His brother glanced back toward Toria's room, then gestured for David to follow him into their room. As soon as they were both inside, he said, "You didn't see Mom?"

David shook his head. "They shot at me again. Xander, they almost got me this time."

"Like they *didn't* before?"

"How are we supposed to get her, when they keep trying to kill us?"

"We gotta find a way. Maybe we're missing something." He moved to his bed and gathered up his pillow and blanket.

David went to his bed. He picked up his pillow and, with one gimp arm, struggled to get the blanket as well.

"Here," Xander said. He tugged off the blanket.

"Thanks. Xander, what you said before, about something worrying you more than the cops coming back . . . ?"

Xander turned, the bedding pressed to his chest with his arms. It made him look like a little kid. "Taksidian," he said. "That guy's not done with us."

"You mean *tonight?*" David closed his eyes. When were they going to get a break? He was exhausted, and he didn't like that being scared was becoming a normal feeling for him.

"I don't know," Xander said. "But I don't think I'm going to get much sleep." He walked into the hall.

At the door, David spotted Xander's mobile phone on the dresser. "Hey," he said, picking it up. "Does Dad have his cell?"

"Usually does."

David flipped the phone open and thumbed a speed-dial number. He listened to the rings on the other end and walked closer to Xander.

"Xan—" Dad's voice said.

Thumps and scratching noises came through to David's ear, then another voice said, "This is Officer Benson. Is this Alexander?"

In the background Dad yelled, "Xander, stay there! Don't—"

David flipped the phone closed. "Oops," he said. "I think the cop just took the phone from Dad."

Xander shrugged. "They would have taken it anyway, at the station. So much for that." He turned away.

"Wait," David said. He pushed the phone into his back pocket. He wanted it close, in case Dad called. He eased the chair away from the linen closet and opened the door enough to peer in. He said, "I should go through."

"Why?"

"Make sure everything's okay."

"That kid knows about the portal," Xander said. "That's not okay."

"We gotta know we can use it, if we have to. You know, *before* we have to."

"What do you think he did, lock it? If he did, and you went through, how would you get back?"

"Taksidian did," David reminded him. "He was in the locker, then went back, without the locker door opening and closing. Must be a way."

"You don't know it," Xander said.

"I can try to figure it out," David said. "If I don't come back in twenty minutes or so, come get me."

Xander scrunched his face. "Go through?"

"No, come to the school and get me out. I don't know," David said. "It may be our only way out, if . . ." He didn't even want to say it. "If Taksidian comes back."

Xander eyed the door up and down as though sizing up an opponent. "All right," he said, dropping the bedding on the floor. "Just there and back. Make sure there's nothing weird."

David opened the door further. He frowned at the interior: shelves of towels and sheets, only enough room to stand in front of them. What if Clayton *had* done something to the locker, something more than locking it? He pictured a fire in it, himself materializing in the flames and unable to get out.

"If you don't want to . . ." Xander said.

David swallowed, feeling the spit slide down his tightened throat. He stepped in and pulled the door closed behind him.

In the darkness, the walls closed in. The floor flexed, buckling under his weight. Metal popped. A scream reached his ears. Had he done that? No . . . not him. Maybe the screech of metal.

The front wall pushed in on him. He cracked his head on the back metal. Something *had* happened to the locker. It was crushed, somehow smaller. If it got any smaller, he'd . . . he'd *implode,* just be crushed with the locker. He elbowed his cast into the side wall and shoved his good arm forward. His hand touched cloth, softness under it.

That scream again—human—followed by sobs, a wretched weeping. Someone sniffed.

David whispered, "Clayton?"

A gasp, more sniffing. "D-D-David?" Fear and panic were in his voice.

David raised his hand. He found a face, wet and gooey. Gross. He wiped it away on his pants. He said, "Clayton, what are you doing in here?"

"You . . . you put me here!"

"I mean, *still*? Why didn't you leave?"

"I . . . I can't!" Clayton said. "I can't get out. And . . . I thought I heard . . . *noises*."

Could he really not find the little tab on the latch assembly that released the door catch? The kid must have been pretty shaken up, zipping into David's house and back again to the locker. True, it was disorienting, but *that* much? Maybe Clayton thought David had sent him someplace else, like a grave.

David had another thought: he had teleported to a place where another person already was. He remembered what his brother had said when he suggested to Xander that they both go through the locker-linen closet portal at the same time: "In *The Fly*, two life forms ended up all mixed together."

What if he and *Clayton* had melded together?

Oh, man!

But that hadn't happened. They'd wound up in the same tight place, but separate and whole. He hoped. He patted his chest, neck, face. No extra parts. Nothing missing.

Clayton said, "What kind of tricks are you pulling on me! What's happening?"

"Clayton, calm down."

David thought about their location: a locker in a short hallway off the main one. Turning left led to the middle school classrooms. On the right would be the cafeteria's doors. Even the janitor would be gone at this hour—otherwise he would have heard Clayton, got him out, and their secret would be blown.

He said, "I'll get you out of here, but you have to promise never, ever to tell anyone what happened. Not about this locker, not . . . Hey, how did you know to get in the locker anyway?"

Clayton sniffed. "When I was after you. I thought I saw the door close, thought I had you. But when I looked, you were gone. Then I heard your freak brother calling for you. I came back to check it out."

"You can't ever tell anyone, you hear?"

"Are you kidding? You are so busted. I'm going to make sure your—your *coven* fries for this, for this witchcraft . . ."

"Okay," David said. "See ya."

"No, wait! Wait! Get me out of here. I was just kidding, really."

"I can put you back anytime I want to," David said as menacingly as he could. "You understand?"

Clayton started crying again.

David felt sorry for him. A little. He thought of something else, just in case the scare tactic didn't work. He reached behind him.

"Hey," Clayton said. "What are you doing? What's that?"

The flash was blinding in the darkness.

David looked at the picture on Xander's cell phone. Tears and snot covered Clayton's terrified face. He turned it for the bully to see, then hit *save* and shifted the phone to his bad hand. He pushed his arm between Clayton and the locker wall, found the catch, and opened the door.

Clayton spilled out onto the tile floor of the school hallway. He flashed a stunned expression at David, standing in the locker.

David snapped another picture. He said, "Stay quiet and these pictures never make it to the Internet. And remember, snot-face, I can put you back in here."

He reached out, grabbed the edge of the locker door, and pulled it shut.

CHAPTER five

TUESDAY, 8:23 P.M.

The kids stood around the island in the kitchen, staring down at plates of soggy spaghetti. David cut away a chunk and forked it into his mouth. The meat sauce didn't help. It still felt like bloated worms on his tongue.

"I gotta go," Xander said. He pushed aside his plate and picked up Dad's keys.

"Don't do it, Xander," Toria pleaded. Spaghetti sauce

coated her lips and face, as though she had tried to put on lipstick while bouncing on a bed.

"We need to know what's going on," Xander said. "I need to talk to Dad."

"You can't take the car," David said, swallowing hard. His stomach threatened to send the food back up—he didn't know if it was the nasty pasta or the thought of being alone with Toria in the house. "You only have a permit."

Xander rolled his eyes. "Driving without a parent in the car is the least of our worries." He picked up his coat and tugged it on. "Look, just stay down here. If anything makes a noise upstairs, run out the front door."

"That cop said they were sending a car over," David reminded him.

"That's why I can't wait around." Xander headed for the door.

David and Toria rushed around the island to join him.

"Take us with you," Toria said.

Xander stopped. He put his hand on his sister's head. "We already talked about this. Someone needs to stay to keep people out. If they bust me, at least you guys will be here."

"Will you get Dad out?" Toria said.

Xander shook his head. "I just want to talk to him."

"You probably won't even get that close," David said. "It's a *jail*."

"David, I know!" Xander said. His shoulders slumped.

"I have to try." He looked out the window beside the door. "No one's here yet. When I come back, I'll park up the road and cut through the trees. Listen for me knocking on the back door, okay?"

David nodded. He thought about saying *If you come back at all,* but it was nothing Xander didn't already know.

Xander opened the door and slipped out.

David pushed it shut and bolted it. Toria gripped his hand. They watched through the window as Xander reached the 4Runner, climbed in, and drove off.

They turned in the foyer and gazed up to the second floor. David remembered the first day they'd found the house. Toria had gone missing, and then her footsteps had seemed to clomp on for a lot longer than they should have.

"Let's . . . uh . . . " He tried to think of something else. If he heard footsteps now, he would drop over dead. "Let's see what else we got in the kitchen."

"There's a lotta s'ghetti," Toria said.

"Great."

They walked hand in hand toward the kitchen, David focusing on the lighted room ahead of them. He was sure, *sure* he would see shadows moving on the second floor if he looked.

CHAPTER

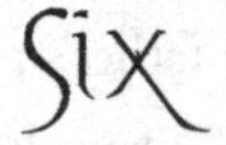

TUESDAY, 8:30 P.M.

"That's *not* what we agreed," Taksidian told the man standing in front of him. They stood in the parking lot of the cabin-sized building that acted as Pinedale's sheriff's office and jail. "All of them out of the house. That's what I wanted."

He rubbed his sharp nails over the scar on the back of his hand. It was all he could do to keep from wringing the man's neck.

Sheriff Bartlett pushed his fingers up under his hat to

scratch his head. The light from a streetlamp cast itself on the man's displeased features. He said, "What we got here, Mr. Taksidian, is a *favor* that went awry. You spoke to the mayor, who suggested we take immediate action to remove that family from the house. But, sir, those aren't the proper channels. If those kids were really in danger, we got *procedures*. There's a child services office over in—"

"I know," Taksidian said. He brushed his long, kinky hair from his face: he knew his gaunt features, thin lips and unflinching eyes were intimidating, and he wanted the the man to get a clear view of them. "That takes days, even weeks, especially considering the father's position at the school."

The sheriff nodded. "They did a thorough background check before he was hired. The man has an impeccable record. No complaints, no—"

"Sheriff Bartlett," Taksidian said with a heavy sigh. "I'm interested only in the children's safety." An image of their freshly covered graves flashed in his head, and he resisted smiling. "I'm sure once they are out of the house and the proper authorities have an opportunity to investigate, they will find evidence of child endangerment. If not from the parents, then from the house itself."

"The house?" the sheriff said, a puzzled look crossing his face.

"I mean, of course, from the condition of the house," Taksidian said. "It's not fit to live in."

"Look, sir," the sheriff said, puffing out his chest. "I was willing to accommodate a request from the mayor, since it didn't seem like such a big deal . . . with the possibility that you're right about the dangers and all. But those kids didn't *want* to come, and physically removing them—Well, that's a whole 'nother matter. That's a line I won't cross, not without a warrant, sir, no way. The only reason we got the father in there"—he hitched a thumb at the jail—"is he accosted one of my deputies. And quite frankly, I don't blame him. Unless you can get child services down here fast, I can't hold him."

Taksidian pointed a gnarled finger at the man's face. He said, "Listen, the mayor—"

A phone chirped.

Taksidian tightened his lips and gave the sheriff his most piercing glare. Keeping his finger up, he removed a mobile phone from his pocket and flicked it open. "What?"

A child's voice said, "Uh . . . is this Mr. Taksidian?"

"What do you want?"

"A friend of mine . . . from school . . . he gave me your number. You stopped him and his friends on their way home. He said you were asking about that old house outside of town. The haunted one?"

Taksidian turned from the sheriff and stepped away. He spoke quietly into the phone. "I was asking about the family who lives there."

"Well, I thought . . . the house, the family—same thing, you know?" said the boy on the other end. "He said you offered . . . uh, money for information?"

Behind him, the sheriff's footsteps crunched over gravel. He was walking back to the jailhouse.

"Hold on," Taksidian said and lowered the phone. "Sheriff?" When the man turned to him, he said, "Keep that man locked up."

Sheriff Bartlett squinted at him. He said, "Mr. Taksidian, I got my deputies heading over to the house right now. I don't want anything to happen to those kids." He paused. "You catch my drift?"

Taksidian glared at him, then turned his back on the man. Into the phone, he said, "What do you know?"

The boy said, "I know how you can get inside. I mean, *secretly.*"

CHAPTER

Seven

TUESDAY, 8:55 P.M.

Ed King sat on the metal cot in the jail cell. His head was lowered into his hands. All he could think about were his kids, left overnight in that house alone.

Overnight? he thought. Who knew how long these yokels were going to keep him locked up? Not for the first time, he wished he could take it all back. He desperately wanted to be in their Pasadena house, his wife and children safe under the roof that had kept the world at bay for years.

His mother had been gone thirty years. What had he been thinking, coming up here to find her? *Bringing his family!* He hadn't even *told* them about the house, the dangers. He had *lied* to get them there.

He slid his fingers onto his head and clutched two fistfuls of hair.

That's when the trouble had started—not when his wife had been kidnapped, but when he had started lying. He had convinced himself that they would have never agreed to moving into the old Victorian—or even to coming to Pinedale—if they had known how dangerous it was. And for what? So he could pursue the crazy dream of finding his mother, a dream—no, a *need*—he had since he was seven years old.

So he'd pretended to know nothing about the house. He'd lied.

He squeezed his eyes closed and tugged at his hair.

What a fool he was.

Now, he'd pulled his whole family into his deceit. He had the kids lying about where their mother was, saying she was in Pasadena, wrapping up the sale of their home. He had taught them to be honest, to live with integrity. Then he had told them to lie, that they *had* to lie.

What a mess he'd made. Everything was spiraling out of control. He had to do something. He had to get them back on track, make everything right again. But what—

Tap . . . tap . . .

He looked around, expecting to see a deputy at the bars. No one stood there.

Tap.

He stood and walked to the bars. There were four cells, two on either side of a short hallway. To his right, a door with a small window led to the sheriff's offices. The tapping came again, and he realized someone was softly rapping on the metal fire door at the other end of the hall, to his left. The knocks took on a pattern, a rhythm he recognized.

Tap . . . tap, tap, tap . . . tap, tap . . . tap, tap.

He smiled. It was the theme from *The Last of the Mohicans,* Xander's favorite movie soundtrack. Every now and then, the boy would play it over and over—in his room, in the car—until the whole family felt as though it was *their* theme, the soundtrack to their lives.

"Xander?" he whispered, then shot a glance to the office door.

The tapping continued.

He noticed a wedge of wood on the floor by the door. He assumed it was used to prop it open when the cells became stuffy.

"Hey!" he yelled, knowing Xander would hear and hoping he'd hide. The tapping stopped. "You, out there, in the office! Hey!" He kept yelling until the office door opened and a deputy stepped in.

"I told you," the man said. "No calls. Not till the sheriff says so, and he just went home, so—"

"Could you turn down the heat?" Mr. King said, tugging at his shirt collar. "I'm burning up." And it was true. He wiped off his forehead and held up his glistening palm.

But the deputy said, "Feels okay to me."

"You want to feel my pits?" he said. "I'm sweating like a fat guy chasing a runaway M&M." He eyed the guy's protruding belly. "Sorry. I'm just telling you—"

"I know, I know," the deputy said. "You're hot." He grabbed the cell door and yanked. It rattled, but didn't open. He went to the fire door, pushed the bar that opened it, and kicked the wedge in place. "Now you're going to get cold," he said.

"I'll yell when I do."

"Don't bother." The deputy went into the office and shut the door.

A few seconds later, Xander's face appeared in the opening. "All clear?" he whispered.

Mr. King waved him in. "How did you know it was safe to knock?"

Xander tiptoed up to the bars. "Movies," he said, as though it were obvious. "The jail cells are always in the back, in a room of their own. That way the deputies don't have to hear the prisoners grumbling or snoring or whatever."

"You were lucky," Mr. King said. "Where are David and Toria?"

"At the house."

"Xander . . ."

"I'll get right back," Xander said. "I told them to stay downstairs, by the door."

Mr. King nodded. "Can you believe this?"

"What are we going to do? Can they just arrest you like that? How long—?"

"It's all garbage," Mr. King said. "I overheard them talking. It's all Taksidian. He got to the mayor. They can't hold me long. First they said we were being evicted, then they said I assaulted one of them."

"But you didn't!"

"Shhh. I know that, and they know that. I think Taksidian just wanted us out for a while so he could plant some evidence in the house . . . or do something to the house that would force us to leave . . . or until he could bribe the right people into issuing a real eviction notice or charge me with child endangerment . . . What are you smiling about?"

"Child endangerment," Xander said. "I think that house fits the bill. And you *did* bring us there."

Mr. King dropped his head.

"Dad, I'm kidding."

Mr. King looked into his son's eyes. He said, "No, you're right. I'm sorry about . . . all of this."

Xander shrugged. "We're in this together now. We can't leave that house until we get Mom . . . and, Dad, I found her!"

"You what? Is she—?"

It was Xander's turn to lower his head. "Well, sort of. David and I went into this Civil War world . . . I know we weren't supposed to, but, Dad, I drew Bob on one of the tents. When we checked again, Mom had left a message. She was there!" He frowned. "We couldn't get to her, but we know where she is, and she knows we're looking for her."

His wife's face filled Mr. King's mind. He blinked and saw his son, looking so much like her. He knew he should be angry that Xander and David had broken their promise never to sneak through a portal again. But that was something they could address another time. Right now all he could feel was relief . . . and gratitude. He extended his hand through the bars. Xander squeezed it tightly.

"Xander," he said. "You're doing it, son."

"But . . . but, what now? You're locked up in here. They're trying to take the house. I don't know what to do."

"Be strong and courageous," Mr. King said. He smiled. He'd prayed his children would be exactly that since they were small. "As you have been."

Xander nodded. He looked toward the office door. He said, "So, what . . . hold down the fort till you get home?"

"You got it." He gave Xander's hand a firm clasp, then let go. He said, "You better leave, before the guy out there comes to check on me. Give your brother and sister a hug for me, okay?"

Xander stepped to the fire door.

"Son?"

Halfway through the door, Xander looked back.

"*Ti amo.*"

It was something they said, picked up from the owners of the restaurant where he had proposed to the future Mrs. King. It meant *I love you* in Italian.

"*Ti amo,* Dad," Xander said, and disappeared.

CHAPTER

TUESDAY, 9:37 P.M.

David heard the knock. He looked through the laundry room to the back door, in the center of which was a decoratively cut window. He didn't see anyone standing there, only shadows from the trees. He wondered if he'd imagined the noise—wanting Xander back so much—or if it had come from somewhere else in the house. He pulled back in.

Toria stared at him with monster eyes.

"No one's there," he whispered. "Didn't you hear—?"

The knock again, a gentle *rap-rap-rap.*

This time a silhouette filled the window. David's heart pounded harder, until he recognized the shape of Xander's shaggy hair.

"What took you so long?" David said, opening the door.

"I came through the woods," his brother said. "There's a cop car out front."

"They showed up right after you left."

They stepped into the kitchen.

"No problems?" Xander said.

"They knocked, but we didn't answer."

"Creaking!" Toria said.

David shrugged. "The house was making some noises. I didn't hear any footsteps."

"I did!" Toria said.

David shook his head. "No, you didn't."

"Did too."

"All right, guys," Xander said. He leaned down to Toria. "This is from Dad." He hugged her.

"You saw him?" David said.

"He said it's all garbage. Taksidian set it up. Dad said it won't stick." Xander looked at David and rolled his head. "I told Dad I'd give you one too."

David hesitated, then smiled. He stepped into his brother's arms.

"Xan-der," David grunted under the crushing pressure. "Not . . . so . . . *tight*." When his brother didn't let up, he brought his foot down on Xander's toes.

"Hey!" Xander hopped away.

"Hey nothing. I got a broken arm, you know."

"Big baby."

David rubbed his arm. "So, what are we supposed to do?"

"Hold down the fort. That's what he said." Xander looked from his brother to his sister. "So that's what we're going to do."

CHAPTER

nine

WEDNESDAY, 12:25 A.M.

Sitting in the passenger seat of the police cruiser, Deputy Sam Parsell gazed through the windshield at the house. It was barely visible through the trees. Its lack of color allowed it to blend into the shadows, seeming to become nothing but shadow itself.

"Creepy," he said. He snatched a Styrofoam coffee cup off the dash and took a sip. He grimaced at its taste, something like cold motor oil.

His partner, Deputy Lance Harnett, sat behind the wheel.

"Holy cow," Lance said. "Listen to this." He held a magazine closer to the dome light and read: "Authorities in West Virginia are investigating reports of unidentified lights in the sky, which correspond with the claims of a Braxton County woman that a 'monster' attacked her German shepherd and ate it. 'It was horrible,' said Nanci Kalanta. 'I went out to see what Killer was barking at. This *thing* ran out of the woods and gobbled him up. One bite, just like that.' Kalanta described the creature as having six or eight legs, a spiderlike body, and a bulbous head with tiny eyes and a mouth 'the size of a storm drain.'"

Lance pulled the magazine down and gasped at Sam. His mouth seemed as wide as the monster's he had just described; his eyes were big and startled. He said, "Can you believe it?"

Sam slapped the magazine out of his partner's hand. "No, I can't. Stop reading that trash."

Lance picked up the magazine. Flipping through it to find his page, he said, "This ain't no gossip rag. It's the *Midnight Sun*, man." He said it the way another person might have cited the *New York Times*. "It's real. They got interviews and pictures and everything."

"Pictures of the monster?"

"Look," Lance said. He pointed at an image of a backyard cluttered with trash. "That's where the dog *used* to be, and look, you can kind of see where the tree branches are broken."

"Gimme that!" Sam grabbed the publication out of Lance's hands. He jabbed a finger into the cover, right into the fanged mouth of what might have been an orc from the Lord of the Rings movies. "What does that headline say? 'Alien Baby Celebrates Third Birthday.' " He threw the magazine at his partner.

Lance looked injured. He said quietly, "You just don't believe."

"You're right, I don't."

Lance rolled up the magazine and pointed it at Sam. "People used to think gorillas weren't real, either." He shook the magazine. "This here is *science.* It's called *cryptozoology.*" He said the word slowly and carefully. "It's the study of creatures we don't know about yet."

"What are they studying, then?" Sam said. He squeezed his eyes shut, mentally kicking himself for opening *that* door.

"Evidence! Eyewitness—"

Sam threw his hands up. "I know, I know. I've heard it already." He looked out at the house. "I can't believe they got us babysitting."

"Well, Sam, them kids are alone in there." Lance's big eyes took in the house, the surrounding woods. "Ain't right."

"Hey, it's their choice. Wouldn't catch me living in a place like that."

Lance turned a big grin on him. "Afraid of *ghosts*?" he said.

"No, I'm not afraid of ghosts. I'd be afraid of rafters falling on me in the middle of the night." Sam opened his door.

"Hey, hey," Lance said, grabbing Sam's arm. "Whatta you doing?"

"I gotta pee," Sam said. "If that's okay with you." He pulled out of Lance's grasp, climbed out, and slammed the door.

Idjut, he thought. He hitched up his pants, adjusted his gun belt, and scoped out the area for a leakworthy spot. The half moon made the house look black and as imposing as an ancient castle. The trees cast deep shadows that shifted as the branches swayed in a light breeze. Mist swirled over the ground, billowing up in the distance. It seemed to glow in the moonlight.

He veered off, away from the front of the house and from where the headlights would catch him if Lance switched them on. As he approached a particularly dark area, a twig snapped somewhere in front of him. He squinted into the shadows.

"Who's there?" he said in his toughest voice.

Something *screeeeeched!*

Sam jumped. His hand dropped to the handle of his pistol.

Screech!

He looked up and saw something moving on the roof of the house. It screeched at him again, and he sighed. It was an old weather vane, mounted to the peak of the gabled roof over the tower. He moved his feet, carefully picking his way over exposed roots and low-lying brambles.

Another twig snapped. He spun toward the sound. It had come from the front of the house on the other side from where he stood.

Animal, he thought. *Had to be.*

He supposed one of the kids could be tromping around, but he and Lance had watched the lights go out more than an hour ago. They had assumed the three inside had gone to bed. He surveyed the front of the house now. No lights.

Something thumped behind him.

Oh, man, he thought, cursing Lance and his talk of ghosts and things that ate German shepherds whole.

CHAPTER

WEDNESDAY, 12:37 A.M.

David woke with a large, warm spider clinging to his face. He brushed at it and realized it was Toria's hand. He lifted it and set it on the pillow between their heads. She mumbled, scratched her nose, and rolled over. She had wiggled toward him until he was teetering on the edge of the mattress. He shifted to his side and gently pushed at her. She didn't budge. He considered joining Xander on the floor, but even a sliver of the bed was better than that.

Bump!

He rose up onto his elbow, listening. Something in the house had made a noise. He heard it again—not a bump this time, but a low creak. Then another.

Footsteps! Or someone trying to walk quietly. His eyes moved to the bedroom door. By the glow of the nightlight he could tell it was still closed. Another creak—out there, somewhere.

"Xander?" he whispered. Louder: "Xander!"

His brother's deep, rhythmic breathing reached him from the floor on the other side of the bed.

He dropped his feet to the floor and stood. Something bumped. He thought about the boxes in the hallway: lots of things to knock into, if you were creeping around in the dark. He went around the bed and knelt in front of Xander. His brother's head was a mass of dark, tangled hair.

David shook him. "Xander, wake up."

Xander shifted in his sleep.

Creak.

David snapped his eyes to the door. He shook his brother harder. "Xander!"

"What?" Xander lifted his head, plopped it back down.

"I hear something," David said. "Someone's moving around out there."

Xander rolled over. He blinked at David, his face like someone in pain. "Someone . . . what?"

"I think someone's in the house."

Xander pushed off his blanket and sat up. He stared at David, listening. "I don't—"

"Shhh," David said.

Ten seconds . . . twenty . . .

Creeeak!

Xander jumped. He got to his feet and pulled David up.

"Where's it coming from?" David whispered.

"In this house, could be anywhere."

"Right outside the door," David whispered. His fear had found its way to his voice.

"I thought maybe . . . upstairs," Xander said.

Great, David thought, *now the house is making each of us hear different things.*

Xander stooped to pick up the toy rifle that had been lying beside him. With a wood stock and metal barrel, it made a sturdy club. He moved to the door.

David grabbed a handful of his brother's T-shirt and followed.

Xander pushed his ear to the wood. He looked back, shook his head.

"Let's go back to bed," David whispered. "Wait till morning."

Xander opened the door.

CHAPTER

eleven

WEDNESDAY, 12:41 A.M.

Sam dropped into the passenger seat of the police cruiser and slammed the door. He glared through the windshield at the house.

"Everything come out okay?" Lance said with a snicker.

"There's something going on," Sam said.

Lance followed his partner's gaze to the house. "Whatcha mean?"

"I heard noises. Like someone walking around in the woods."

"The kids," Lance suggested.

Sam didn't speak for a while. He scanned the woods in an arc, starting where Lance's head blocked his view and ending with the passenger-side window. Finally he said, "*Maybe* the kids. But I went up on the porch, checked the door. It was locked. If it was one of the kids, the door wouldn't have been locked."

"Back door, then." Lance's eyes were the size of half-dollars.

Sam could tell he wanted a straightforward explanation for the noises. The guy might get a kick out of reading about boogeymen, but he didn't want to end up in the *Midnight Sun*'s next issue under the headline Sheriff's Deputy Mauled to Death by Alien Dog-Boy.

"Maybe," Sam said, not believing his own word. All the breaking twigs and thumps had come from the area in front of the house. Kids would have run off when Sam had started exploring, and he'd have heard them making tracks toward the back. "I think I'll—"

Something smacked down on the roof of the cruiser.

Lance screamed. He fumbled for his pistol.

Sam grabbed the man's arm. "Don't," he said. "If the kids are out there . . ." He didn't even want to think of what could happen if Lance started plugging away at the shadows.

"That's no kid," Lance said. "Something landed on the roof."

Sam scowled at him. "What are you thinking? Something *living?*" He shook his head. "A rock maybe."

"It was big," Lance said.

"Well, I don't hear anything now. Nothing's moving up there."

"Waiting."

"Hey," Sam said. "A light just turned on in the house. I can see the windows on either side of the door. Couldn't see them before."

They watched the house, but nothing else happened. No more lights, no movement.

"Turn on the headlights," Sam said.

Lance squeezed his eyes closed and flipped on the headlights. The woods between the end of the road and the house sprang into Sam's vision. The nearest trees seemed to glow in the brightness. Farther trees caught their shadows and appeared to multiply as they approached the house. The lights barely reached the front porch steps.

"Hit your spotlight," Sam said, reaching for the handle on his side of the car. The brighter spots, Sam's and Lance's, came on at once. New shadows snapped into place. Sam's roamed over the right side of the yard—if that's what you'd call the woods in front of the house—Lance's over the left.

"There!" Lance said.

The leaves of a large bush were shaking.

"Wind?" Lance said, hopefully.

"Not the way it's moving back and forth like that."

The shaking stopped.

"Hold the light on it," Sam said. He positioned his own light on the porch and opened the door.

"Wait!" Lance said. "The roof."

Sam stepped out, rising slowly to peer at the roof. A large branch lay over the cruiser's red-and-blue light bar. He looked up. The top of the tree leaned out over the car's hood. He grabbed the branch and showed Lance.

"See?" he said. "Probably just fell. Keep your eyes peeled." He shut the door and headed for the woods. His shadow stretched out in front of him, reaching almost to the house.

CHAPTER twelve

WEDNESDAY, 12:50 A.M.

"Xander!" David said. He was standing at the junction of the second floor's main hallway and the smaller one that went to the room they were using as a Mission Control Center.

Xander was shining a flashlight on the secret door at the end of the short hall.

"It's still latched," Xander said, running his hand over the wall.

"There are lights shining in from outside," David said. The glow flickered in the main hallway, brighter than the dim overhead fixtures.

Xander stepped up beside him and switched off the flashlight. He brushed past David, who once again grabbed hold of his brother's shirt. Xander edged closer to the staircase.

"Is it the cops?" David whispered.

As Xander eased forward, the light caught him, flickering like a fire. He said, "Probably. But what are they doing?"

"Maybe they spotted something," David said, thinking of the creaking floorboards.

They stopped at the top of the stairs. The light was coming through the windows by the doors. Something moved in front of the beams, causing a bobbing shadow. It grew larger and darker. The porch stairs creaked.

"Xander?" David said.

Xander sidestepped behind the wall. They both crouched low. Xander craned his head around the corner; David bent around Xander to see. The shadow took the form of a person: head, shoulders, arms. Footsteps clumped on the porch. The door handle rattled. The person moved to the side window and peered in. He was silhouetted with light radiating from behind.

Xander pulled back behind the wall. He nudged David. "Get Toria," he whispered. "We have to be ready to get out of here."

David looked down the hallway to the chair that they had replaced under the linen closet handle. "The closet?" he said.

"That's the plan," Xander said. "Now, go."

CHAPTER

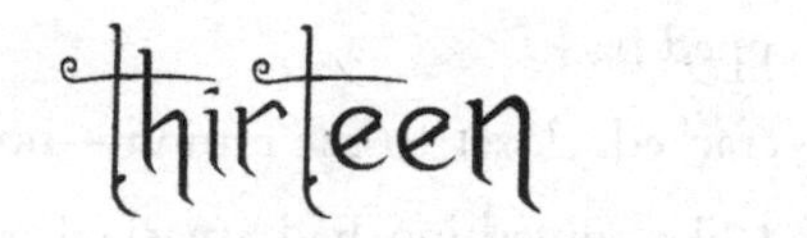

thirteen

WEDNESDAY, 12:52 A.M.

At the window, Sam cupped his hands against the sides of his face. The upstairs lights were on, but he didn't see anyone. The rest of the house was dark. The door was still locked. Probably one of the kids had gone to the bathroom. He turned away from the window.

The cruiser's lights glowed at the end of the road like a four-eyed spider waiting to pounce. Mist snaked slowly from the side of the house, swirling around trees and billowing up against the bushes.

He looked at the big clump of bushes Lance's spot was on. From his perspective it was mostly a shaggy black mass. He went down the steps, treading softly. As he approached the bush, it shook.

He stopped. "Who's there?" He unsnapped his holster and moved closer. "Trinity County Deputy," he announced. "Come out with your hands up."

The bush rattled. Something growled, low and guttural.

Sam stepped back.

A twig cracked, closer to the cruiser—no, no, not a twig. It sounded like something had smacked against glass. He squinted at the car. Had Lance got out? The thing in the bushes growled again.

A loud *crack!* came from the cruiser, and Lance's spotlight blinked out.

What in tarnation?

"Lance?" he called.

A screech made his blood run cold. He swung his head around. That blasted weather vane!

The headlights and his own spot were pointed not at the bush, but at the house. The bush was now illuminated only by the backsplash of light bouncing off the ground and trees. Somehow that made it appear even darker, bigger, and a whole lot scarier than it had looked in only the moonlight.

The leaves rustled. That deep-throated growl reached his ears, getting louder.

He pulled his pistol. "I got a gun," he said. "You hear me?"

Movement drew his eyes to the side of the house. The mist drifted among the trees. Sam's breath froze in his lungs. The clear shape of a man stood rock-solid near the rear of the house.

"Who's that?" Sam said. "Come here . . . slowly."

The figure didn't move.

Sam swung his gun toward it. "I'm not kidding, buddy!"

The bushes shook. The growling continued.

Sam held the gun on the unmoving figure and raised his free hand to shield himself from whatever might rush out of the bushes. He didn't know what to do. He wasn't going to shoot at the figure: Not when the guy wasn't even moving. Not when there were kids around, and he couldn't be absolutely sure the figure wasn't one of them—though the man in the mist seemed a lot bigger, more *solid* than any kid he'd ever seen.

Still . . . should he approach the creepy dude? That would put his back to the bushes—and whatever was in them.

Behind him, he heard the car door open.

"Sam!" Lance said. "Sam, get back here, man! Get out of there!"

That decided it. He took a step back. The ground here was spongy with soft soil and decomposing leaves. He began to tumble, caught himself, and shuffled in reverse.

The car door slammed shut. The trees erupted in flames—that's what Sam thought for a few seconds, until a blue light pushed away the red and he realized Lance had turned on the police flashers. The red light swung around again. Blue. Red. Blue. They flashed against the trees but didn't reach the figure in the mist. To Sam's eyes, they made everything worse, making shadows jump up and fall back. He couldn't tell what was real movement, from which he had to protect himself, and what was merely the dance of light and shadow. He swung his gun between the bushes and the figure and backed away, backed away.

His own shadow became blacker and sharper on the ground as he neared the car. When his heels touched the dirt road, he spun and ran for the passenger door. He hopped in, panting. He scanned the woods through the windshield. He thought the figure was gone, but it was hard to tell, between the darkness way back there and all the lights doing their thing.

"What's going on?" Lance said. He sounded panicked.

Sam looked over at him. The door window behind Lance's frightened face was broken: a dozen cracks fanned out from a small hole in the glass. "What happened?"

"I think someone shot at me! They hit the light!"

"Get us out of here," Sam said. "Come on, start the car!"

Lance cranked on the key. The engine roared. He slammed the shifter into gear, and the cruiser reversed away from the woods.

Sam watched through the windshield, half expecting something to chase them. He held his pistol up, ready. "Did you call it in?" he asked.

"No, I—" Lance grabbed for the radio.

Sam clutched Lance's hand. "Forget it," he said. "Just go, go."

"But—"

"What are we going to say?" Sam said. "That we got scared away?"

"Someone shot at me!"

"That's not a bullet," Sam said. "See the way the glass is crushed around the hole? I've seen it a hundred times. It was a rock."

"Then why are we taking off?" Lance turned the car toward the side of the road and put it in drive.

Sam realized Lance had not seen the figure or heard the growling. He said, "Because I don't know what's going on here, but it ain't no good." He shook his head. "It ain't no good."

"What about the kids?"

"If they're the ones throwing rocks, they don't deserve our protection," Sam said. "If they're inside, they're safe."

"You sure?"

"Sure enough. Go, will ya?"

Lance accelerated, kicking gravel up into the wheel wells, sounding like angry rattlesnakes. He swept the car around and got it pointed away from the house.

Sam turned in his seat to watch the blackness through the

rear window. Lance braked, casting red light on the road behind them and the trees on both sides.

Then the car rounded a bend, and Sam relaxed. He closed his eyes and sighed. He said, "I never did like that house."

CHAPTER

fourteen

WEDNESDAY, 1:05 A.M.

Keal watched the police car vanish around a curve. He crunched across the forest floor and stopped next to a bush.

"For Pete's sake, Jesse," he said. "I should never have let you talk me into taking you out of the nursing home. You didn't say anything about throwing rocks at cops."

The bushes laughed, a thin coughing sound. Hiding behind them, the old man said, "I haven't seen people move that fast since someone passed gas in an elevator."

"It's not funny," Keal said, but he laughed a little in spite of himself. He shook his head. "It's one thing for me to fly you across the country because you think the folks in this house are in danger. It's something completely different to attack police officers. I'm just saying, you better know what you're doing."

"Oh, pooh," Jesse said from behind the bushes. "Wasn't us who scared them away. It was the house, this place. We just helped it out a bit. Now, don't just stand there. I got a stick jabbing me in the back."

Keal made his way around the foliage. The shadows here were even darker than the rest of the woods. He couldn't make out anything.

Jesse wheezed in a breath, and Keal moved faster. He was supposed to take care of the old guy. Didn't matter if it were back at Mother of Mercy Nursing Home or here, Jesse was his responsibility.

He said, "You okay?"

"Nothing I'm not used to," Jesse said. "These old lungs don't work the way they did once." His laugh sounded like sobs. "Nothing does. *Owww!* You stepped on me."

"Sorry," Keal said. "Can't see."

He knelt down, running his hands over Jesse's scrawny body. He cupped his hand under Jesse's head. When he lifted it up, a stray beam of moonlight caught the old guy's face. He was smiling.

"Now, that was fun," Jesse said.

"I wasn't laughing, man," Keal said. "That cop pointed his gun at me. I was sure I was a goner. And he was heading right for you."

Jesse growled.

Even watching the old man make the sound, it put goose bumps on Keal's arms and the back of his neck. "That's just freaky," he said.

"It worked," Jesse said. "Did you see that guy hightail it for his car?"

"I'll give you that one. You all right?"

"Just tired," Jesse said. "Not used to being up so long. I feel like . . ." His lids drooped. "Like I could just . . ." His eyes closed, his mouth fell open, and he snorted in some air.

"Yeah, funny . . ." Keal leaned closer. "Jesse?"

Jesse's eyes sprang open. He smiled. "I ain't *that* tired . . . or old. You going to get me off this cold ground or what?"

Keal got his arms under Jesse and lifted him. It was like picking up a scarecrow, the man was so light.

Jesse said, "I gotta admit, I wasn't expecting the gun."

"They're cops, Jesse. What *did* you expect?"

He felt the old man shrug.

Jesse said, "Smooth move, putting out the light, my friend. And with only two throws. You missed your calling. You should have been a pitcher."

It was Keal's turn to shrug. "Spent some time in the minors. I'll tell you about it someday." He crunched over the ground cover, carrying Jesse toward the front of the house. He stopped.

In the distance, mist was billowing up between the trees, glowing in the moonlight. In front of the slowly stirring cloud stood a man, silhouetted against the mist. His shoulders rose and fell as though he were breathing heavily.

"Jesse?" Keal whispered.

Jesse caught his stare and followed it. He let out a deep sigh.

"Who is it?" Keal said quietly.

"One of *them,*" the old man said. "I knew it had started again."

"*What* started, and *who* . . . ?" Before Jesse could answer, Keal called out, "Hey! What do you want?"

The dark figure backed into the mist and disappeared.

Keal waited, but the man did not reappear. He heard no sounds from the woods besides the wind and an occasional squeak from the weather vane.

"A watcher," Jesse said.

"Watcher? What's he watching?"

"Us. The house. Everything that happens here."

Keal didn't move.

Jesse said, "Never mind him, Keal. If he was going to do anything, he would have done it. He's only someone else's eyes."

"*Who* someone else?" Keal moved his attention from the

mist to Jesse's face. He was surprised to see not even a hint of concern in the old man's features; only sadness.

"Could be anyone," Jesse said. "This place, what it does, has always attracted . . . *outsiders,* people who don't belong, who want to use it for their own wicked intentions."

Keal could not find the words for all the questions zipping through his brain.

"What'd you think," Jesse said, "that a house like I told you about could possibly exist and *not* draw the likes of him and whoever he answers to?"

Keal looked for the man again. Nothing but trees.

"Let's get on with it," Jesse said.

Unsure, Keal carried Jesse to the porch steps and lowered him. He glanced around, stopping on the windows flanking the doors. He said, "Lights on inside. Someone must be home."

"Well, I should hope so," Jesse said. "I came to see them, not *this* place."

"Those cops'll be back, you know. With an army."

Jesse shook his head. "Not if they're anything like the ones I knew back when. They didn't want anything to do with the house."

"Let's hope they still don't," Keal said, nervously scanning the woods on both sides. "Still, why do you think they were here?"

"Never can tell," Jesse said. "Always something *interesting* happening 'round here."

"I guess so," Keal said. "I should get the car."

They had pulled it behind some bushes around the bend.

"That can wait." Jesse opened his eyes. "We got business to attend to." He raised his eyebrows. "I can use my chair, though."

Keal started to walk off. He stopped. He couldn't keep his eyes from darting around. "Why don't I take you with me?"

"Because then you'll have to carry me *and* the chair." Jesse waved him away. "Go, go. The worst that will happen is someone will watch me sitting here growing older."

"I wish I felt as confident as you sound."

"Keal," Jesse said with a sigh. "You could have been back with the chair by now."

"Okay, okay. Wait here."

"What else am I going to do?"

Keal trotted into the woods. He came back with Jesse's wheelchair, folded up flat. He sprung it open, scooped Jesse off the steps, and eased him into the chair.

Jesse leaned his head back to take in the imposing facade before him. "I thought I was done with you," he whispered to the house.

CHAPTER

743 BC

TIYARI MOUNTAINS, NEAR NINEVEH, ASSYRIAN EMPIRE

Raindrops struck Dagan's face, as biting as lions' teeth. He blinked against the onslaught, determined to reach the cave above him before one of the lightning bolts that cracked through the black sky blasted him off the mountain. He paused in his ascent, lowering his head to breathe without water rushing into his throat. The narrow ledge he had been traversing before spotting the shelter lay twenty meters below. Currents of rain sluiced over it, becoming drops again as the water flowed over the edge into a bottomless ravine. In the space of a thousand heartbeats, the ledge had become impassible.

At least the other boys wouldn't be able to get ahead of him. Not while the storm-god Adad was so angry. Perhaps one of them would try; certainly, the stakes were high enough to make them consider an attempt.

The academy to which they belonged instructed its pupils in the arts of death: stealth, infiltration, and murder. The best of them would graduate into the most elite rank of the great Assyrian war machine, that of Assassin. Every year the academy sent all of its students sixteen years of age on a grueling, five-day trek from Nineveh to Autiyara, equipped with only the clothes on their backs and a blade. The first one to arrive continued his studies. The runner-up became his lifelong servant, sharpening his weapons, cleaning his clothes. The others were consigned to the regular army as front-men, fodder for their enemies' spears.

As he had been since his recruitment into the academy on his eighth birthday, Dagan was the best in his class, and he was ahead of the others now. But Amshi, his dearest friend since the two had endured the initiation rites together eight years before, was not far behind. Always a close second, Amshi was Dagan's only real competition in this latest challenge. The thought of becoming Amshi's servant—of not becoming an assassin himself—made Dagan sick, as though a serpent had made a home in his guts.

But that isn't going to happen, *he thought. Not by the war-god Nergal would Dagan allow himself to lose.*

He turned his face up into the pounding rain. Beyond the cliff to which he clung, gray clouds roiled, expelled from Adad's mouth like poisonous vomit. Lightning flashed down, momentarily blinding the boy. He pushed himself higher toward the cave, making sure each rock he grabbed was secure. If he fell, his blade would never taste human blood, and that was unacceptable. How could he spend eternity in Irkalla saddled with that kind of shame?

At the lip of the cave, the wind whispered his name. He stopped, listened.

" . . . Dagan . . ."

A million raindrops crashed into the stone cliff, roaring like a crowd welcoming home a triumphant army. Dagan strained to hear . . . he was sure he had heard . . .

" . . . Dagan . . ."

From his perch just outside, he peered into the darkness of the cave, then at the empty air around him. That's when he saw Amshi down on the ledge, squinting through the rain at him. The boy, Dagan's age but much younger looking, gestured back the way they had come, probably to a more accessible shelter.

Dagan shook his head, scowled at his friend, and pulled himself into the cave. He crawled a few feet in and collapsed onto the gritty floor, panting. He was amazed at how good *it felt to be out of the incessant pounding. He rose to his hands and knees and went back to the cave's mouth. He stuck his head out, felt the rain like a swarm of insects, and saw the top of Amshi's head. The boy was following, scaling the cliff toward the cave.*

Dagan returned to the dry darkness of the cavern. Gritting his teeth, he cursed his friend. He knew full well what Amshi was doing: he had realized the futility of trying to progress along the ledge, and since he had to stop, why not do it where he could keep an eye on Dagan, the only one who posed a threat to his reaching Autiyara first? Amshi would rest well, knowing the competition was not pressing on.

The serpent inside Dagan coiled around his heart.

He moved farther into the cave, found a fissure in the wall, and pressed himself into it. He listened to the storm outside, to water dripping from his hair to the stone floor, to his breathing, growing slower.

His hair had dried by the time he heard Amshi heave himself into the cave. The boy did what Dagan had done: he crumpled to the ground and waited for his breath to return. Then he called, "Dagan?"

Dagan heard him getting to his feet, stepping deeper into the cave.

"Dagan? Where are you? Are you hurt? I found an overhang out of the rain, but this is much better." He drew closer. "Dagan, where—?"

Dagan emerged from the fissure. His arm shot up.

Amshi jumped, caught sight of Dagan, and smiled, a wide boyish grin. Then it vanished as he saw the object Dagan held slicing through the air toward him.

And for the first time, Dagan's blade tasted human blood.

••••••• ••

The cramped darkness in which Dagan—now Taksidian—stood reminded him of that initial kill, so long ago. He thought of Amshi—not the playmate who'd laughed when their voices cracked at the onset of manhood, who'd eased the tension of a trying day on the training fields with a whispered joke—he thought of the body he'd left in the cave. It would have decayed, even the skeleton becoming powder after so many millennia.

Taksidian squeezed the hilt of his knife. The weapon had made him the assassin he was, the man he had become. And on more than a few occasions, it had saved his life. It was his friend, more surely than Amshi ever had been. His blade had feasted many times since that first taste. Now it was hungry again.

For the dozenth time, he checked the door. The handle turned, but the door wouldn't open. He tried to quietly shoulder his way through, but whatever held it was strong. He was about to return to the locker in the school when he heard noises beyond the door, in the hallway.

He leaned his ear against the door. Soft footsteps. Quiet voices. Something was going on out there, in the house. He shifted his feet into a more comfortable stance and leaned back against the shelves. He would bide his time in the closet a little longer.

He would await the opportunity for his blade to feast again . . .

CHAPTER

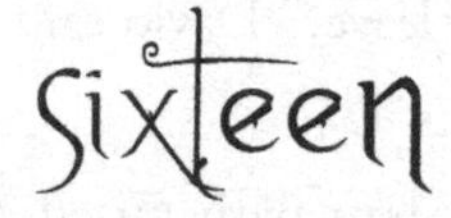

WEDNESDAY, 1:16 A.M.

David led Toria into the hallway by the hand. She was half-asleep, mumbling something about going on a ride. Her free hand clutched her "nigh-night," a threadbare baby blanket she always slept with. She stumbled and stopped, seeming ready to doze standing up.

"Come on, Toria," David said.

Xander was on all fours in the hallway, peering around the corner to the foyer below.

David realized the lights were no longer shining through the windows. "Did they leave?" he whispered. He knelt beside his brother and leaned to see the front doors and the windows beside them.

"I don't know. A car left, but I just heard voices out front."

"Where are the policemen?" Toria said. She had plopped down behind the boys and now blinked heavy lids at them.

"I think they were the ones who left," Xander said. "There were red and blue lights flashing through the windows, and now they're gone."

"Why would they leave?" David said. "And if it's not the cops out there, who is it?"

Xander looked at him with raised eyebrows. "Who do you think?"

"Taksidian?" David's chest grew tight. It seemed that no matter how many times something frightened him, he never got used to it.

Footsteps clomped heavily on the porch steps.

Xander backhanded David in the arm. "Come on," he said. "Let's get to the other side of the stairs before they get to the windows."

David reached back for Toria, but she was already rising. They darted past the staircase and the railing that overlooked the foyer. Where the wall started again, opposite Toria's bedroom, they dropped to the floor. Xander looked around the corner and through the railing to the front door.

Toria nudged David. She said, "Why did Xander want us on this side of the stairs? Aren't there more hiding places on the other side? We could go up to the third floor."

"Xander," David said. "Toria doesn't know about the closet."

With all their discussion of the closet-to-locker portal, let alone their use of it, it was difficult to believe it had remained a secret.

Xander smiled at her. "If we have to run, you're in for a big surprise."

"I don't like surprises," she said.

Xander shook his head. "Then you live in the wrong house." He turned his attention back to the front door.

Something banged down on the porch. There was a squeak, somehow different from the weather vane, which had been reaching David's ears every now and then since he'd awakened.

He rose on his knees to see the front door over his brother's head. A shadow moved over the tall, narrow windows. Both he and Xander pulled back.

"I have to go to the bathroom," Toria said.

"Can you hold it?" David said.

She bit her lower lip and shook her head.

"Make it fast, Tor," Xander said.

Bam! Bam! Bam!

David jumped and grabbed Xander's shirt again. "They're *knocking?*" he said.

"Pounding," Xander corrected.

"Taksidian can't expect us to answer."

"David," Toria called quietly. She was standing in front of the bathroom, pointing at the chair in the hallway. "What's *that* doing there?"

Xander swung his head around. "Don't touch it," he said. "It's part of the surprise. Go, if you have to. Hurry."

"And don't flush," David said.

Toria made a face and disappeared into the bathroom.

The pounding on the door continued.

"What if it's the cops?" David said.

"We're still not answering."

The door handle rattled.

Now David's stomach tightened and rolled. It felt like one of the cannonballs he had recently seen.

Somebody spoke, the deep voice of a man. David could hear the rhythm, but he could not make out the words. A second voice, quieter, responded.

Bam! Bam! Bam!

"Hello?" the deep voice called. "Anybody in there?"

David said, "I don't think that's Taksidian."

"I don't care who it is," Xander said. "It's after one in the morning, we're alone, and people are out to get us."

A thump followed by scraping echoed from the door.

"What's that?" David said. His fear was morphing into panic.

"They're trying to break in," Xander said.

The boys scrambled up and headed down the hall. Xander stopped and reversed so quickly, David lost his grip on his brother's T-shirt.

"What—?" he said, then he saw the toy rifle Xander had left on the floor.

Xander snatched it up, hefting it in his hands.

"Wish it was real," David said.

Toria came out of the bathroom.

"We're leaving," Xander told her. He pointed at David. "You go first. Get out of the locker as fast as you can. I'll send Toria next."

Thinking of Clayton's experience, David said, "I can open the door for her from the outside, when I hear her come through."

"Come through?" Looking up at them, Toria's eyes were big and scared. "What locker? Where are we—?"

Xander put his hands on her shoulders and leaned his face close to hers. "The people outside are trying to break in. Just trust us, okay?"

David watched her searching for reassurance in Xander's eyes. She must have seen it: her features softened, and she nodded.

Something banged against the front door—not a knock. But David realized with some relief it wasn't the door crashing open, either.

David and Xander looked at each other, drawing strength from one other.

"Okay," David said. He gripped the closet door handle as

Xander bent to pull the chair away. Under David's hand, the handle moved—all by itself. He lunged at Xander, knocking him away from the chair. The toy rifle clattered away.

Xander hit the wall, and they both went down.

"What are you doing?" Xander said.

"There's someone in the closet!" David said. "Where's the flashlight?" He spotted it on the floor on the far side of the grand staircase. He planted one hand on Xander's chest and pushed himself up. He ran past the foyer and the stairs, certain the door would burst open.

He grabbed the light and ran back. Toria saw him coming and flattened herself against the wall. David dropped to his knees, then flat on his stomach, in front of the chair. He switched on the flashlight and shined it beneath the door: *shoes!* They were black. They shifted apart as their owner adjusted his stance. The right one rose out of the light. A heavy crash rattled the door as the person inside kicked it.

"Xander!" David yelled.

Xander was already leaning over him to brace his arms against the back of the chair, which in turn pressed against the door. The handle shook, and the door rattled under the impact of another kick.

While David watched, the shoes appeared to evaporate. They lost their shape and melded with the blackness around them. A feather-light breeze touched his face . . . was gone . . . then blew out from under the door again. In time with the pulsing breeze, the flashlight beam stuttered. It didn't flick on and off, but seemed to be *consumed* by the draft. Between flickers, the shoes disappeared.

David panned the light back and forth along the empty floor, while Xander continued leaning his weight into the door.

Finally David said, "He's gone."

"You sure?"

"Pretty much." He scooted away and stood.

The front door creaked open.

CHAPTER

Seventeen

Wednesday, 1:23 a.m.

Jim Taksidian stepped out of the locker. The school hallway was dark. The only light came from the moon through the windows. He leaned backward, stretching his spine. He bent, pulled up his right pant leg, and slipped his knife into the sheath strapped there. He straightened and ran his fingers through his long hair, smoothing it and tucking it behind his ears. He turned back to the locker. It looked just like all the others. But of course it wasn't, just as the house wasn't like any other house.

He shut the locker door and touched the little plate riveted to it: 119. Good to know the number, finally.

He walked around the corner and down the hall. His footsteps were silent on the tiled floor. His fingers massaged the heavy scar on the back of his right hand. Even after all these years, it still ached: sometimes it merely throbbed in time with his heartbeat, but occasionally it felt like a white-hot wire pressed into his flesh.

He welcomed the pain. It reminded him of the injury, the last time anyone had spilled his blood. The prince's guards had fought valiantly. They had nearly killed him, in fact. But in the end, it was they—and the prince—who had paid the ferryman. Taksidian had survived, and he had accidentally discovered the portal that brought him to the house. *From assassin to king,* he thought, thinking of the fortune he had amassed since then. *Not a bad trade.*

He pushed through the double doors at the end of the corridor and turned left. He stopped beside the glass exit doors and punched in the code that would reactivate the school's security system, giving him thirty seconds to leave. It never stopped amazing him, what people would tell for the right amount of money. Slipping the janitor two hundred bucks had bought him unimpeded access to the school, day or night.

He pushed through the doors into the central courtyard. The air was crisp, turning his breath into plumes of mist. He gazed up at the half moon, the same one he'd wondered about as a young man, before the rise of the Roman Empire. He strolled across the grass toward the boy waiting for him on a picnic table. The boy was young: not yet a teenager, but close. He had his feet propped on a bicycle, rocking it back and forth.

"Well?" the boy said.

Taksidian scanned the dark windows of the school, the forest beyond, and the parking lot. He slipped a hand into the pocket of his black overcoat and withdrew a wad of cash, peeled off a few bills and held them out. His eyes wandered the sky; watching the boy accepting the money was just so . . . *crass,* like witnessing a dog devour a rabbit.

"Hey," the boy said, "you're short."

Taksidian turned his eyes on him. He stared until all of the boy's confidence had drained away like blood from a slaughtered pig.

The boy lowered his eyes. "I mean . . . it's just . . ."

Taksidian's voice was deep and flat. "The closet door was locked."

"What?" The boy's eyes went wide. "You couldn't get in? How was I to know? It was open before." His tone had risen, panicked now—not for the money, but for what Taksidian might do to him for wasting his time.

Fear was an emotion Taksidian appreciated in others. It had

serviced him well over the years. He ran the thick, sharp fingernail of his index finger over his bottom lip.

The boy stared at it.

Taksidian reached out. His fingernail grazed the boy's skin as he flicked a lock of hair off the boy's forehead. "What scares you?" he asked.

"What do you mean, what scares me?"

Taksidian stared into his eyes. "What haunts your nightmares?"

The boy melted under Taksidian's gaze. He said, "Vampires." He swallowed. "Snakes."

Taksidian leaned close. He whispered, "The deadliest snake in the world is the Inland Taipan. A single bite contains enough venom to kill a hundred full-grown humans. But it's a puppy dog . . . compared to me." He let his breath wash over the boy's face, then he backed away. "As for vampires, they have nightmares about *me*."

He let that sink in, then said, "Do you understand?"

The boy nodded.

"Forget about the Kings and their house. Forget about the locker. Forget about me."

The kid was shivering, but Taksidian was sure it had nothing to do with the cold.

He smiled. "Of course, if you learn anything else, I want to know about it."

The child nodded again.

Taksidian turned away, then spun back around. He leaned over and ran a fingernail along the side of one of the bicycle's tires. "What did you say your name is again?"

"C-C-Clayton."

The tire popped.

Taksidian smiled. "That's so you have plenty of time walking home to think about what I said."

CHAPTER

eighteen

WEDNESDAY, 1:23 A.M.

The door downstairs thunked open. Footsteps moved from the porch into the foyer.

David's eyes jumped to Xander, leaning against the closet door. He heard Toria pull in a breath, and he clamped his hand over her mouth before she could scream.

Eeek-eeek. A squeak like the weather vane, but this came from downstairs. The chandelier hanging over the foyer came on.

Someone said, "Shut the door, Keal. Don't want our friend outside to wander in."

A voice smooth as a sports announcer's said, "I thought you said he was only watching."

The other man mumbled something David couldn't make out. The door closed.

The smooth voice called, "Hello? Anyone home?"

"What do we do?" David whispered, so quietly even his own ears didn't hear.

Xander nodded at the linen closet door.

"No," David said, louder. "Taksidian—or someone—just went through. He'll be there."

"Then we have to use one of the doors upstairs, one of the time portals."

Toria pulled David's hand off her mouth. "I don't want to," she whispered. "I don't want to go through a portal."

David couldn't blame her, with all the stories she'd heard from him and Xander.

Xander pushed himself off the closet door and put his face in front of hers. "We have to," he said. "These people want to take us away. Then who will rescue Mom?"

A voice came at them from the foyer. It was fragile and quavery, as though the speaker were sitting on a paint shaker. "I can hear you," the voice said. "I'm not the bad guy. I'm here to help."

Toria's eyebrows shot up, and she smiled.

Xander frowned. "What else would he say? 'Come on down so I can kill you'?"

David heard that same *eeek-eeek* again. He got a crazy vision of a pirate standing in the foyer, his wooden leg squeaking every time he moved. In this house, he wouldn't be surprised if the person downstairs actually turned out to be a pirate.

"I know about the portals," the shaky voice continued.

"See?" Xander said. "Has to be one of Taksidian's men."

"I know that one of you saved a little girl in World War II."

Xander's eyes flashed wide. He gaped at David.

David's lips moved, but they found no words. Finally he said, "How . . . ?"

"Huh?" Toria said. Her face reflected complete bafflement. "What little girl?"

David started for the grand staircase.

"Dae, no!" Xander grabbed his arm.

"Taksidian can't know that," David said. "Only you, me, and Dad."

Xander thought about it. He released David's arm and stood.

David took a step, and his brother grabbed him again.

Xander said, "Be ready to run."

David said, "Straight upstairs, right?"

"Right." Xander gave Toria a firm look.

David walked slowly, willing that ferret in his chest to settle down. He took a deep breath and stepped up to the banister that overlooked the foyer. A big black man stood, staring up at him. He was standing behind an ancient geezer in a wheelchair. The old man was mostly bald, except for a cloud of white hair circling around from one temple to the other. He had a thick silver mustache and eyes so blue David could see them sparkle, even from a floor away.

The old man spotted him and squinted. His lips pushed into a radiant smile.

David felt hope rush through him, as though his blood had warmed by a couple degrees: the man had the kindest face he had ever seen.

"I should have known," the old man said. He shifted in his chair to smile up at the guy standing behind him. "I should have known." He started coughing. It was a wheezy, raggedy sound.

The other man put his hand on the old man's back. He leaned around to watch his face as he coughed. He said, "Jesse? Jesse, you all right?"

The old man—Jesse—fluttered a scrawny hand in the air. When he looked up at David again, his eyes were wet. He said, "I can't tell you how wonderful it is to see you again . . . David."

David took a step back and bumped into his brother.

"And *you*! Xander."

David said, "How do you know us?"

The wrinkles on Jesse's face rippled and hardened in a posture of concentration. He said, "Let's just say that *I* have met *you*."

Toria stepped up to the banister.

Jesse said, "Oh . . . and who is this?" He wheeled his chair back for a better look. One of the wheels creaked. *Eeek-eeek.*

Toria told him her name.

Xander said, "How do you know David and me, but not our sister?"

"It's a long story, and I hope to have the time to tell it." He glanced around. "Please tell your parents I'm here."

"They—" Xander started, then stopped. "What are you doing breaking into our house?"

"I'm sorry about that," the old man said. "We wanted to call, but information gave us a 626 area code. That's not around here."

"That's our old number," David said. "In Pasadena. We just moved in."

The old man nodded. "Information didn't give a new one. We drove straight from the airport. I . . . I wanted to get here as soon as possible."

Xander said, "So you just barged in?"

Jesse looked up at them sheepishly. "Keal did knock."

"Well, you can just wheel yourself right back—"

David elbowed his brother in the ribs. Hard.

Xander yelped.

David whispered, "There's something about him, Xander, can't you tell? I think he's on our side."

"Dae, they *broke in!*"

The two boys looked over the handrail. Jesse was grinning as though he was the guest of honor at a surprise party.

"Who *are* you?" Xander said.

"Name's Jesse. This is my friend Keal."

Xander leaned against the railing. "I heard, but *who are you?*"

"Unless I've miscalculated . . ." Jesse closed one eye as though he were struggling through a math problem. "I'm your great-great-uncle."

CHAPTER

nineteen

WEDNESDAY, 1:27 A.M.

David, Xander, and Toria stared down at the old man. They looked at one another.

"Come on," Xander said. He slapped David's arm, grabbed his sister, and practically carried her down the hallway, out of sight of the intruders.

David's gaze connected with Jesse's. Something about the kindness David saw in the old man's face made him want to return it, however vague and unsupported by action it was. He held up his index finger. He said, "Be right back."

"Take your time," Jesse said.

When David reached Xander and Toria, he said, "I like him."

"You don't know him," Xander whispered. "If we're related, how come we've never met him before? How come we've never even heard of him?"

Toria skewed her face. "How's he *related* to us?"

"It'd be like . . ." Xander closed one eye, thinking, and David thought he looked an awful lot like Jesse at that moment. "Dad's dad's dad's brother. The brother of our great-grandfather."

"Or great-grandmother," David said.

From downstairs, Jesse called, "Great-grand*father*."

Xander grabbed David and Toria's arms. He walked backward down the hall and into the boys' bedroom. "It's too weird," he said. He looked at David. "Why is he showing up now, and how does he know us?"

"Maybe he's on Mom and Dad's Christmas card list," David said.

"Then he would've known Toria too," Xander said.

"What are you saying?" David asked. "He's an imposter? Why?"

"To get in with us," Xander said, as though it were obvious. "A spy. I wouldn't put it past Taksidian."

"If Taksidian sent them," David said, "why would he try to break in through the closet at the very same time?"

Xander's frown said *Good point.* "To scare us, show us how much we need an ally."

"We already knew that," David said.

Dad had told him that in old times when criminals were stoned to death, it didn't always mean having rocks thrown at them. Just as often, a condemned man would lie on his back, and a board was placed on top of him. Then people piled stones on the board until the collected weight crushed him down so firmly, his lungs could not expand and he would suffocate. The King family problems felt like that . . . like being crushed to death.

David said, "We need a *break,* Xander. Ever since we moved in, it's been one bad thing after another. Why can't something good happen for once?"

"Yeah," Toria chimed in. "Why can't Jesse be here to help?"

"Maybe because he broke into our house?" Xander said. "At one thirty in the morning? Hmmm . . . yeah, that's normal."

"Nothing about this house is normal," David said. "When help comes, it'll *have* to be not normal."

"David, you're being—" Xander stopped. He put his hand on David's shoulder. "You're right, we do need help. I just don't want to be . . . I don't know, so desperate for it that we take anything or anyone who comes along."

"Can't we just talk to him?" David said. "Figure out if he's telling the truth?"

Xander nodded. He said, "Okay, but we stay together."

In the hall, Xander picked up the toy rifle. They stopped at the top of the stairs. Keal was kneeling beside Jesse's wheelchair, one hand resting on the old man's shoulder. David noticed for the first time how pale Jesse looked. It made the moles—"age spots," his dad had once told him—on Jesse's hands, face, and scalp stand out all the more.

"All right," Xander told Jesse and Keal. "Go into the dining room, to the far side of the table."

Jesse's brow furrowed. "What about your parents?" He read their expressions. "Aren't they here?"

"That's none of your business," Xander said.

The old man nodded, and Keal wheeled him into the other room. *Eeek-eeek-eeek.* Chairs scraped against the dining room floor.

Xander went down the stairs, David and Toria moving right behind him like parts of a caterpillar. Xander wielded the makeshift club over his head and peered around the corner of the dining room before he walked in.

Jesse and Keal were sitting behind the table. Their hands were folded in front of them on the flat surface as though patiently waiting for dinner.

David brushed past Xander and took the chair opposite Jesse. The old man stared at him intently, but there was nothing mean about it. It was the way Mom and Dad looked at him sometimes—there was love behind it. But it *was* kind of odd to think that this stranger would *love* him.

Toria sat beside David. Her eyes darted between the two men. David figured she was doing what he'd already done: sizing them up, noting how different they were from each other, but somehow a team.

Like us, he thought.

Jesse noted David's broken arm resting on the table. He studied David's face, the black eye and bruised cheek. "You guys look like you've been in a couple scrapes."

When they didn't respond, he cleared his throat. "I can tell you're very capable children, and I am a guest in your house . . ." He looked each of them in the eyes. "But it's not right that I'm here, talking to you without your parents."

"Well, all right, then," Xander said. "See ya."

"No, wait!" David said. He grabbed Xander's T-shirt. "Xander, please."

His brother frowned. He told Jesse, "Don't worry about our parents right now. We want to know more about *you.*"

"Fair enough," Jesse said. "What do you want to know?"

"How did you get in?" Xander said. "The door was locked. Dad just had it rekeyed."

"Oh," Jesse said, "I know a few tricks about this place."

David said, "How did you know about the little girl in World War II?"

"That was you, right?" Jesse said. "The one who saved her?"

David nodded. "There was a tank—"

"And you grabbed her before it ran her over," Jesse said.

David's mouth fell open. "How . . . ?"

He looked at Xander, who was scowling at the old man.

"Two days ago, I woke up and the world was different," Jesse said. "I mean, it had *changed*. You, David—you changed it."

CHAPTER

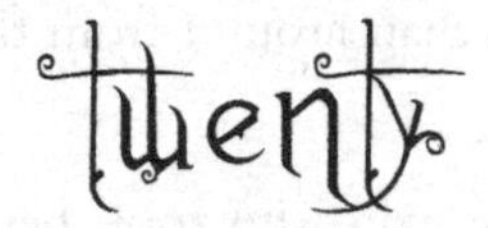

Wednesday, 1:41 a.m.

"What do you mean, I changed the world?" David said.

Jesse rubbed the silver stubble on his checks. Folds of skin moved under his fingers. He said, "I'll show you." He reached over his shoulder, groping for something on the back of the wheelchair.

Keal reached behind Jesse and produced a manila envelope. He handed it to the old man.

"Thank you, Keal," Jesse said, flipping open the flap. He pulled out a piece of paper and slid it across the table toward David.

It was a photograph showing a farmhouse in the background. In front was a family posing for the camera: a man, a woman, and a little girl.

David gasped. He picked it up and squinted at it. "That's her," he said. He showed it to his brother. "Xander, that's the girl I saved from the tank!"

Xander took the photo, looked at it closely, then handed it back. He slid the chair around from the end of the table and dropped into it.

David said, "The man who took her from me said her name. Marge . . . Mag . . ."

"Marguerite," Jesse said.

"Yeah."

"Marguerite Rousseau." The old man fished into the envelope again. He withdrew another piece of paper and said, "Do you know what smallpox is?"

"Like chicken pox?" David asked.

"Much worse. Blisters and a rash cover the skin, inside the mouth and throat. Very unpleasant. That's the common variety. Then there were the more severe strains. My friend Jeffrey Lewis was much younger than I. He was one of those people who kept you young just by being around, he was so full of energy. He contracted the hemorrhagic form of the disease on a mission trip. His skin turned black from all the bleeding of his organs and muscle tissue." Jesse looked at Toria. "I'm sorry, sweetheart. Let's just say he suffered terribly. Jeffrey died on September 12, 1994."

"Wait a minute," Xander said. "I thought smallpox—"

Jesse held up his hand to stop him. His eyes were wet. "You have to hear this," he said. "Earlier today, I spoke to my friend. I spoke to Jeffrey Lewis."

David jumped as if Jesse had lunged out of his chair at him.

"What?" Xander said. "You talked to a guy who *died* in 1994?"

Jesse nodded. "At the airport in Chicago. Keal made the calls for me."

"Tracked the guy down," the younger man said. "When I made the connection, I put Jesse on."

Jesse said, "I had a wonderful conversation with him. He's retired now. Wanted to tell me all about his grandkids."

"You just said he died," Xander said, obviously irritated.

"He did," Jesse said, "in the world that existed three days ago. In today's world, he never died. He said the worst illness he ever had was a stomach bug years ago. I asked him."

"That's . . . *impossible*," David said.

Jesse said, "In the world you know, it is, but here—"

"Besides," Xander interrupted, "I learned about smallpox. It's been gone for . . . like forever."

Jesse agreed. "The World Health Organization declared it

eradicated on May 8, 1980." He put the envelope and paper on the table and pressed his hand over them as though preventing them from flying away. "A couple of days ago, I had memories I no longer have. I wrote them all down." He tapped his fingers on the paper. "I remembered the world—today's world—still suffering from smallpox. Two million deaths a year. The disease spared no one: children, parents . . . anyone could contract it, and an average of six in ten of those who did died of it." He panned his eyes across the faces of the King children.

"So you had a dream," Xander said.

"It wasn't a dream," Jesse said. "It was a memory."

"You probably remember polio too," Xander said.

Jesse shook his head. "You don't understand. It was a memory, because three days ago, that's the way the world actually was. Smallpox had not been wiped out. *Two* days ago smallpox was gone—and had been gone for thirty years."

"That doesn't make sense," David said.

Jesse smiled. "Three days ago Marguerite Rousseau had died as a child, a casualty of the German war machine. But two days ago, she hadn't died—because *you* saved her. She grew up to perfect the vaccine that eliminated smallpox from our world."

Xander sighed loudly. He leaned back and ran his fingers through his hair. "Like I said, I learned about how we beat smallpox when I was in seventh grade, three years ago. It didn't just change a couple days ago."

"It did and it didn't," Jesse said. He tilted his head toward one shoulder, then the other like a clock's pendulum. "The world changed when David saved Marguerite. That happened for David two days ago; it happened for Marguerite nearly seventy years ago. Everything became different the moment David saved her, the moment in *history* when he saved her."

"I don't get it," Toria said.

"Time travel is tricky business," Jesse said. "Scientists argue about it. Most say it'd be impossible to change history, because the past is the past."

"But you know better," Xander said.

Jesse's head went up and down, slowly.

David pressed his chest into the table's edge. "I still don't get how you knew it was me who saved her and it was at that moment that history changed."

"Some of us have a gift," Jesse said. "We *sense* those changes. When the change occurs, the way things were *before* the change comes to us like a dream or almost-forgotten memory. After a couple of days, even *that*—the dream, the memory—fades. Then we're like everybody else: we don't remember that the world was ever any different. When I woke the other day, smallpox had been eradicated years before. But I had memories that it hadn't been. I knew someone had changed history. That's why I wrote my thoughts down—before they left my mind for good."

He stopped, raising his head to listen to something David didn't hear. Then he did hear it: the house was groaning, a low, steady sound that reminded him of the way the trees around the house creaked in the wind.

Jesse winked at him and said, "This house has old bones too."

David smiled. He hoped that was *all* it was.

Jesse went on. "Right now, I have no recollection of smallpox during the last forty years. I have no memory of Jeffrey Lewis's death. But I have what I wrote." He picked up the page, shook it, and set it down again. "I used a computer to research smallpox. I learned about Marguerite. In her autobiography, she details her childhood in the French village of Ivry-la-Bataille. I have an excerpt here."

"Oh, come on," Xander said. He stood abruptly. "What's the point?"

"Xander," David said, pleading.

"You want someone to read to you, Dae, I'll go get Grimms' fairy tales. It'll mean as much." He pointed toward the ceiling. "Mom is—" His lips clamped shut. He shifted his gaze to Jesse.

The old man cocked his head, waited for Xander to continue. When he didn't, Jesse said, "You might want to stay for this, Xander. Ms. Rousseau writes about your brother."

CHAPTER

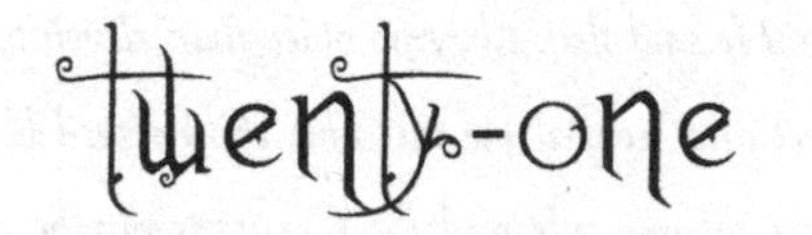

twenty-one

WEDNESDAY, 1:50 A.M.

Xander blinked at Jesse. "She wrote about David in her autobiography?"

"Published in 1988," Jesse said.

"I wasn't even born yet," David said.

Xander appeared uncertain. Slowly he sat and scooted the chair forward.

Jesse consulted the paper. "Marguerite tells how her town

was destroyed when the German army came through. Her father was a Resistance fighter and died there. Her mother was also killed."

David looked at the lady in the picture. She could have been the woman he'd seen fall in front of the tank. His heart ached for her.

Jesse said, "Her uncle raised her. He told her how she had almost died as well during the attack. Here's what she wrote." He squinted at the page, a shaky finger moving over lines of text. *"The tank was bearing down on me. My uncle was too far away to help. He said that a boy no older than eleven or twelve darted out into the street and scooped me up. This child risked being shot by the Resistance fighters on one side and the Germans on the other. When he grabbed me, the tank was but a meter away. I sometimes think what that boy must have felt at that moment: the heat from the tank blasting his skin; bullets flying around him, sparking off the tank; the smoke of burning buildings and ignited gunpowder stinging his nostrils, burning his lungs. And yet he saved me. My uncle claimed to have never seen this boy before or since. This is very strange, considering Ivry's small community."*

Jesse glanced up.

David blinked. His chest was tight, remembering.

Jesse said, "I think you'll like this next part. *I have often wondered about this child's bravery, and how he seemed to come out of nowhere and then return to nowhere after saving my life. I have come to this conclusion: he was an angel."*

David's breath caught in his lungs, and he grinned. He

swung around to see Xander's stunned face. He said, "An *angel.*" He turned to Toria. "Did you hear that?"

She said, "You? That was you? Wow!"

Looking at her, David felt as though he had grown two inches taller, with broader shoulders—if not for real, then at least in his sister's eyes. He remembered the shrapnel that had hit his calf, how badly it had stung. He thought of how scared he had been, so close to puking from fear. He could almost feel the flames he had run through to get to the portal that took him home, and how the fire had burned his shirt collar. All of these things seemed to fall away from him now, like heavy rocks he had been carrying. He had saved someone who had gone on to save millions. All that meant, to himself and to the world, was too enormous for his mind to grasp.

Jesse said, "That's how I knew *when* the world had changed. A long time ago, I took to recording my dream-memories in a journal. Sometimes these memories would leave me so suddenly, I had to stop writing in midsentence. I used to read that journal every now and then. It kept me from forgetting what it was all about."

"What *what* was all about?" Xander said.

"This house."

"Can you . . ." David said. "Can you help us?"

Xander stood and grabbed David's arm. "We have to talk."

David smiled apologetically. He followed Xander into the foyer.

"What are you thinking?" Xander whispered.

"You mean, after everything you heard, you're still not ready to trust him?"

Xander rolled his eyes. "He said some people have a gift to know when history changes. Okay, I'll buy that. This house proves that anything's possible. That doesn't mean he's a good guy."

"Xander, *please.*"

His brother looked around, thinking. His eyes settled on the upstairs hallway. He whispered, "What would Dad do?"

"He'd say yes to help," David said. "If it meant getting Mom back faster, he'd say yes. You know he would."

Xander nodded. "All right. Let's see where this leads." He pointed at David. "But don't tell them about Mom. Not yet."

"But—" David started, not sure how they were supposed to get help without saying what they needed help doing.

Xander's stern expression made it clear the point was nonnegotiable.

He gave in. "Deal."

They went into the dining room. Toria's head rested on her arms, which were crossed on the table. Her hair covered her face and spilled over the edge like a waterfall. Her back rose and fell gently.

"She's out," Keal whispered. "This one might be faking." He gestured toward Jesse.

The old man was slumped in his chair, his chin on his chest, snoring.

"Faking?" Xander said.

"Yeah, he likes to tease."

David knelt beside the wheelchair to examine Jesse's face. The old man's lids were closed, eyes moving behind them, the way they do when you dream. His mouth was slightly open, and his bottom lip vibrated with every drawn-in breath.

"Jesse?" David whispered. He looked at Xander. "He's *sleeping.*"

"Figures," Xander said.

"But we were gonna . . ." David wasn't sure what it was exactly they were going to do. "*Tell* him . . . ask for his help." It sounded lame, not at all the Obi-Wan Kenobi moment his gut told him it was.

He frowned. The pressure to rescue Mom before something happened—to her, to them, to the house—felt like juggling dynamite. He wanted so badly for someone to step in and lend a hand, to snatch the explosives out of the air and give his arms a rest.

"Do *you* know what's going on?" Xander asked Keal.

"With the house? Him and the house? Some."

"What about him and the house?" David said.

"He *built* it," Keal said, as though they should have known. "His father and brother and him."

David swung his head toward Xander. Both of their mouths hung open, both of their brows furrowed tight.

"He should have said that in the first place," Xander said.

"He'd have gotten around to it," Keal said. "This man's head is like a library—especially when it comes to this house. But you can only read one book at a time."

"When did they build it?" David said.

Keal tightened his face, trying to remember. "I think . . . 1932, '33? He was a teenager. About your age, Xander."

"He must know *everything* about the house," Xander said. "All of its secrets."

"I don't know about that," Keal said. "The way he talks, it's like . . . like the house has a life of its own. Your mom and dad know a lot about you, but not everything. And the older you get, the more things you take on that are your own: experiences, dreams, fears. Seems to me this house is like that."

David didn't want to hear that. They needed for the man who built the house to know all about it, to tell everything they needed to know to beat it.

A hint of disappointment must have shown on his face.

Keal said, "But between the building and the living in it, he's gotta know something, don't you think?"

"How long was he here?" Xander said.

"I think something like . . . forty-five, fifty years."

"*In this house?*" David couldn't even imagine being here that long. He studied Jesse's sleeping face. The adventures he must have had.

The house groaned again, and David knew immediately it wasn't simply "old bones." The sound grew louder and deeper, like the start-up of an engine big enough to power a city. Sharp sounds seemed to signal the splintering of wood, the cracking of glass, but he saw nothing like those things.

Jesse startled awake. His eyes darted around. His hair was buffeting around his head. It snapped out and froze, pointing past his face at the foyer. It unfroze and billowed, as if in a strong breeze. His shirt collar started to flap.

David was kneeling beside Jesse's wheelchair, and he didn't feel a thing. He raised his hand and moved it in front of Jesse. Nothing. He touched his own hair: flat on his head as it should have been. Xander's too: shaggy and uncombed, but not moving.

Jesse said, "I have to leave."

"What? No!" David said.

Jesse's hair went limp.

The groaning and cracking faded until the house was silent again.

"What was that?" Toria said. She blinked sleepily.

The old man said, "The house is talking to us."

"What's it saying?" David said.

Jesse looked down at him. He put his hand on David's arm, which David had draped over a wheel of the chair. His eyes were intense, fire blue, like Dad's and Xander's.

Jesse said, "It's hungry."

CHAPTER

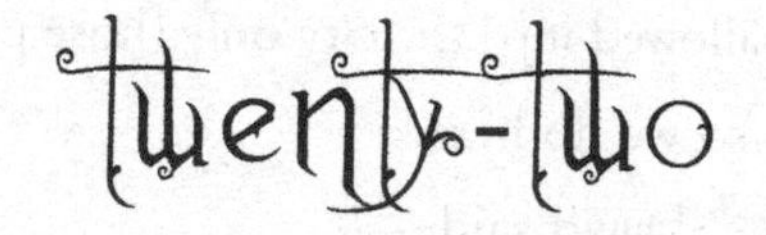

WEDNESDAY, 2:07 A.M.

Oh, come on! That was the last thing David wanted to hear: *It's hungry.*

Jesse laughed, an airy wheeze. He patted David's arm. "Don't look so scared, son. It's not just an ordinary house, but I can tell you that you're more than an ordinary boy. You and Xander—your family—you're *meant* to be here."

David shook his head. "I don't understand."

"This house, those rooms upstairs," Jesse said. "It's what we do. It's in our blood. Our society has grown away from it, but there was a time when whole families, generation after generation, knew what part they played on life's stage. Hunter, leader, blacksmith . . . we're all gifted to do something very specific. Not everyone finds out what that is, but it's true. In some cases, like ours, it's in our lineage, it's what this *family* is supposed to do."

"What?" David said. "What are we supposed to do?"

Jesse leaned closer. "We're *gatekeepers,* David. The way gatekeepers of old allowed into the city only those people meant to be there . . . so we do here."

"We do *what*?" David said.

"We make sure only those events that are *supposed* to happen get through."

"To where?" David said.

"To the future."

David looked to Xander, but his brother looked as baffled as David felt.

The house groaned mournfully.

Jesse's hair fluttered. "I have to leave," he said again.

"But . . ." David gripped the old man's shoulder. It felt like nothing but bone under the jacket.

"I'll be back tomorrow," Jesse said. "I promise."

"I was hoping . . ." David said. "I was hoping you'd stay. I mean, in the house with us. Sleep here. We have room."

"I wish I could," Jesse said. "But I've been into those other worlds so many times, they think I'm theirs."

"Theirs?" David said.

"The worlds'. Time's." Jesse scanned the ceiling. He said, "I can feel the pull. I can feel it wanting to drag me back into the stream, the stream of Time. That wind blowing my hair? That's it, grabbing at me. If I stay in the house too long, it'll just—"

He snapped his fingers, inches from David's nose, making him flinch.

"*Snatch* me away, just like that."

"But we need your help," David said.

Jesse put his hand on David's head and brushed his hair back. "And you have it," he said. "I'll be here as much as I can, for as long as you want me. But when I feel the pull, I'll have to go away for a while. Not long: few hours, few days—I don't know. That's the way it has to be."

David frowned. "Okay . . . I guess."

Somewhere in the house a door slammed. All of them jumped, and Toria let out a quick scream.

Jesse took his eyes off the foyer entrance to address the children. "Keal and I are going to a motel in town." He frowned. "If you want, if you'll feel safer, I can get a room for you there too. At least until your parents return."

"We can't," Xander said. "We can't leave the house. Not now."

Jesse appeared disappointed. "Well," he said, "I think it's

acting up because I'm here. You'll be okay." He smiled, pushing up the edges of his mustache.

If he says "I think" now, David thought, *I'm outta here. Motel, here I come.*

But Jesse said no more. He nodded at Keal, and the big man stood.

••••••••

David and Xander watched through the windows on either side of the front door. Jesse sat on the edge of the porch while Keal carried the wheelchair through the woods to the road.

"His hair's doing it again," David said. It was billowing around his head the way it had done in the dining room. It snapped back toward the house, then forward, as though catching in the ebb and flow of a tide.

"Look beside him," Xander said.

Within Jesse's reach was an elm leaf. It was big and dry and papery looking in the porch's light. On his other side was a clump of pine needles. Neither the leaf nor the needles so much as fluttered.

"It's only him," Xander said, "feeling the wind."

David said, "The way his hair is blowing one way and then the opposite, it's like the house is breathing."

"Great," Xander said. "Like it's not creepy enough. Now it talks and breathes."

"And it's hungry," Toria said from her perch on the stairs.

David made sure the door's dead bolt was locked. He said, "What do you think about what he said, our being gatekeepers?"

"I think he's crazy," Xander said. "*I'm* not supposed to be here. We're going to find Mom and get out of here. As soon as I'm old enough, I'm heading back to L.A. to make movies. Maybe I'll make one about this house. That'll be all the gatekeeping *I'll* do." He looked up toward the second floor. "We gotta go get Mom."

"*Now?*"

"She's waiting for us, Dae."

"I can't, Xander," David said. He was whining, and he didn't care. "I'm beat. Let's start again in the morning."

His brother glared at him. "It's not fair," he said. "We *found* her. She was *right there.* I thought all we had to do was get you in there to show her the way home."

"They chased me away," David said.

"I know, I know." Xander slapped his hand on the ball atop the post at the base of the banister. "Then everything happened to keep us from getting back to her! It would have been better if we'd never seen her message."

"No, I'm glad about it," David said. "It's nice to know she's safe, and she knows we're looking . . . More than looking; we're *close.* I don't know how these worlds work. She went in one, came out and back in another, and now she's in an even different one.

But, Xander, she's going to do everything she can to stay in the Civil War world until we get to her. I know it."

Xander nodded, looking at their sister sitting on the stairs.

Toria's eyes were closed. Her head rested in her hands, and it kept drooping to one side, then snapping back up.

"Okay," Xander said. "Tomorrow, for sure."

"For sure," David agreed, already starting to doze off.

CHAPTER

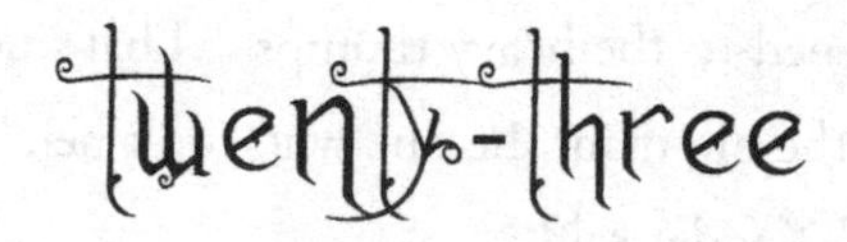

Wednesday, 2:42 a.m.

David and his sister lay shoulder to shoulder in Toria's bed. Xander was on the floor beside it. All three stared at the ceiling. The paint had peeled in spots, and a few water stains marred its surface. David was sure there was more damage to the ceiling than he could see by the dim glow of Toria's Fiona nightlight. But it didn't matter. What had them all unable to sleep, on edge and frazzled, was the clomping around up there. Footsteps pounded, objects clattered. For the umpteenth time, David lifted his head to make sure the chair was still wedged under the handle of the closed bedroom door.

He rolled onto his side to see Xander and whispered, "We could move into our bedroom."

"Do you really want to go into the hallway?" Xander said.

David didn't answer. After a while he said, "Good thing we didn't go up there to look for the Civil War stuff."

"I've been thinking," Xander said. "What if it's Mom making that noise?"

David listened to the heavy thumps. "That's not Mom," he said. "It's the big man, the one who took her."

"Phemus," Xander said.

"What?"

"There was a poster at school. It shows Odysseus being captured by a Cyclops. The Cyclops is huge and muscular, but a little flabby too. He's naked, except for these animal pelts around his waist. And he's bald."

"Sounds exactly like the big man," David said, amazed. "Does the Cyclops have a beard?"

"Naw, that part's different."

"Plus, the big man has two eyes," David pointed out. "He's not a Cyclops. What's Phay-mus?"

"Phemus," Xander corrected. "The Cyclops's name is Polyphemus. I call him Phemus for short. That's the guy who took Mom."

"Phemus," David said, feeling it on his tongue.

It sounded like something was being dragged through the third-floor hallway.

"I'd like to know what's going on," Xander said.

"You're not thinking about going up there?" David got a cold chill just thinking about it.

"Are you kidding?"

"I don't want anything to do with that hallway when whatever's making those noises is there. Phemus or whoever. I'd rather never know what's going on and live, than find out and die."

"No, *really*?" Xander said.

David rolled away.

Toria's eyes were closed, her mouth slightly parted.

He settled onto his back. A minute later he whispered, "Good night, Xander."

"'Night, Dae."

David's eyes felt heavy in his head, grainy as though sand had gotten in. Every time he blinked, it took more and more effort to open his lids again. Toria's slow, deep breathing lulled him closer to sleep. The noises from the third floor faded—in reality or only in his own ears, he didn't know, and didn't give it much thought.

His eyes closed and stayed that way.

CHAPTER twenty-four

WEDNESDAY, 9:48 A.M.

His mother woke him. Her hand gently shook his shoulder. His eyes fluttered open. There she was, leaning over him. The morning light radiated behind her.

"Mom?" With consciousness came excitement: She was here! She had found her way home!

"David?" she whispered.

"Mom!" He sat up, throwing his arms around her. *I missed you! I love you! Are you all right?* But none of these things came out.

He just wanted to hold her, squeeze her, feel her in his arms.

"David." She pushed him away.

His eyes found her face, longing to see it.

He blinked. The corners of his mouth dropped, as did his heart.

Toria sat in front of him, her face contorted by concern. She said, "Are you all right?"

"I—" Unwilling to let his mother go, he looked around the room. Daylight through the window made everything clear—and it was clear his mother was not there.

"You're crying," Toria said. She brushed her fingers over his cheek.

"I thought . . ." He blinked, wiped his eyes.

"I know. You thought I was Mom," Toria said. "You were dreaming."

He tried to smile but couldn't.

His sister's face brightened.

"What?" he said.

"I want to go," she said.

He took a deep breath and let it out slowly. He shook his head. "Until Dad sorts things out with the police, we can't leave the house. They might grab us and not let us back in."

"No," she said. "I mean, I want to go get her. I want to go over."

He glared at her. "Who? You? You said last night you didn't want to go through a portal."

"I changed my mind. For Mom. You said they chased you out."

David said, "The first time we went to the Civil War, I was wearing Confederate gray." He saw that she didn't understand. "Xander and I—and Mom—were in *Union* territory. They thought I was an enemy soldier."

"Xander too?"

He shook his head. "I guess they thought he was a Union soldier trying to run away. They don't like that much."

"But they don't know *me*," she said, "and I'm a little girl. What are they gonna do?"

"You don't know these worlds, Toria," David said. "It's almost like the people over there *look* for reasons to not like you, to want to hurt you."

"But I have to go, Dae."

"Go where?" Xander said. He put his hand on the bed and lifted himself up to sit beside Toria.

"She wants to go over."

"No way," Xander said. He gave their sister a little push. He squinted at David. "Were you crying?"

Again David wiped his eyes, his face. He said, "That's . . . something else. Toria knows we can't go back, but she thinks she can."

Xander stared into the corner of the room, thinking. He nodded.

"Xander, no," David said.

Xander raised his eyebrows. He said, "Maybe she's right."

"It's too dangerous."

"*We* made it out alive."

"Barely," David reminded him.

"Look at her," his brother said. "Who's going to hurt anything so cute?"

Toria grinned.

"Dad would kill us," David said.

"Not if everything goes all right," Xander said.

"Yes!" David grabbed Xander's arm. "In this case, even if she gets Mom and comes back without a scratch, he'd kill us. You know he would."

CHAPTER twenty-five

WEDNESDAY, 10:30 A.M.

The argument continued in the kitchen.

David dropped bread into the toaster. He said, "It's never gone smoothly for us when we go over. It's always about fighting, running, survival."

"Not all the time," Xander said. He was scrambling eggs in a frying pan. "There was that one peaceful world. Beautiful meadows. Even the animals weren't afraid of me. Dad and I threw rocks into a river."

"That sounds nice," Toria said. She was opening a package of bacon for Xander to fry up.

David watched the coils inside the toaster turn orange. He said, "*One* place where people weren't trying to kill us. One. And we *know* the Civil War world. It's not a peaceful meadow."

Xander scooped the eggs onto a plate and started laying strips of bacon into the pan. The sizzling meat sounded like gale-force rain striking the windows.

The smells reminded David how hungry he was. The night before, he had choked down maybe three bites of clumpy spaghetti, which had sat in his stomach like Play-Doh.

Tongs in hand, Xander watched the bacon. He said, "Crispy or fatty?"

"Crispy," Toria said.

David said, "I don't know about 'fatty,' but I don't like crispy." The toast popped up, and he transferred the slices to a plate. He put more bread in the toaster, levered them down, and began buttering the finished ones. He said, "I can't believe we're doing this."

"Arguing?" Xander said. "Hey, you're the one who won't listen to reason."

"I mean making breakfast," David said. "Like it's just some normal day."

"Maybe it is," Xander said. "For us."

The toast kept tearing under David's butter knife. Every stroke made the bread uglier. He turned away from it.

"Dad told me, 'Time is God's way of preventing everything from happening at once,'" he said. "But it *is* all happening at once: We have to rescue Mom from a world that's trying to kill us. We have to figure out how to get Dad out of jail without letting them arrest us too. We have to watch out for Taksidian and the fifty ways he's trying to capture us, murder us, or otherwise get us out of the house. We should be picking Jesse's brain for everything he knows."

"Picking his brain?" Toria said. "*Eew.*"

"It means learning what he knows, Toria," David said. "My point is, it's too much, all at once."

Xander smiled at him. "Like I said, maybe that's our normal . . . now that we're in this house."

"I wish we'd never laid eyes on it," David said.

Xander flipped the bacon. He said, "I'm not sure we ever had a choice, Dae."

"What do you mean?" David said. "Like it's our *destiny* to be here?"

Xander shrugged. "I'm just saying. With Dad kind of making it happen, and the reason he did going back to when he was a kid. And remember, we were excited about this place . . . attracted to it, even though it was scary. Doesn't all of that feel like destiny to you?"

"What about Hollywood? You said you were going to make movies."

"I am. This is today's destiny. Filmmaking is tomorow's."

The second round of toast popped up behind David. He said, "I don't know what destiny feels like, but if this is it, I don't like it. I want to un-destiny this place from my life."

"That's why Toria should go over," Xander said.

David wanted to punch him. "Xander, it's too—"

Xander waved his hand at him. "Never mind, never mind. You know those noises last night, the ones coming from the third floor?"

"Creepy," Toria said.

Xander began using the tongs to pull the bacon from the grease and lay the strips on folded paper towels. "David, you said you'd rather not know what was causing them than go up there and die."

"And you said, 'No, *really?*'" David reminded him. He put the new toast on top of the mangled slices, then cut thin patties of butter from the stick and set them on the edge of the plate. He carried his breakfast contribution into the dining room.

Toria followed with the eggs, and Xander with the bacon.

Xander said, "What if I figured out a way to know what's happening without having to go up there?"

David gave him a puzzled look. "Okaaaay . . . ?"

"A camera," Xander said. A big grin stretched out on his face. "We put one right at the beginning of the hallway, just inside the landing."

David followed Toria back into the kitchen. Xander was

right on him, wanting David to tell him what a brilliant idea it was.

Instead, David said, "Will a camera work up there? Your video camera didn't work when I took it over into that jungle world."

"That was through a portal," Xander said. "Who knows why it went wacky? I've filmed all over the house. It works."

Toria brushed past them, carrying three glasses of OJ. David picked up a stack of plates, and Xander plucked forks out of a drawer.

"So what?" David said. "You start filming when we go to bed, then check it in the morning?"

"That's no good," Xander said. "It doesn't record that long, and I want to know what's happening when it happens, not later."

"So what are you thinking?" David passed out the plates and sat down.

"Security cameras," Xander said. "Those wireless ones that show the camera's perspective on a TV or computer monitor."

Thinking about it, David scooped eggs onto his plate and dropped three strips of bacon beside them.

A forkful of eggs was halfway to his mouth when Toria said, "David . . . ?" She was reaching her hands out to him and Xander.

David set the fork down and clasped his siblings' hands. When no one said anything, David gave Xander's fingers a squeeze.

Xander said, "Heavenly Father, thank You for this food. Please keep Mom safe and bring her home soon."

David stepped in before Xander could close the prayer. He said, "Dad, too."

Xander said, "And make us strong and courageous. Amen." He smiled. "Last night, when I saw Dad in jail, he said that's what we have to be."

"He always says that," David said, nodding. He leaned over his plate and began shoveling scrambled egg into his mouth like coal into a furnace.

"So, anyway," Xander said, "the hardware store sells security camera kits."

"Aren't they expensive?" David said.

"Don't talk with your mouth full," Toria said. "Gross!"

David opened his mouth wide.

Toria lowered her eyes to her plate.

"I've got money," Xander said.

"You do?"

"Mom showed me some cash she'd set aside to buy me a car."

"You're kidding." Everything about that amazed David: that their parents had extra money and that they'd put it into a car for Xander.

It wasn't that they didn't *want* to buy their kids things, but teaching—as Dad had done before accepting the principal's position here in Pinedale—wasn't exactly a high-paying career. And Mom had chosen full-time parenting over juggling a job and kids, so that's what she had done since Xander was born.

They were always pinching pennies for little extras, like David's soccer equipment and Toria's piano lessons.

But a car? *Wow.*

"She was so cool about it," Xander said, remembering. "She wasn't going to tell me until my birthday, but she knew the move was getting me down, and she hoped it would cheer me up."

David nodded. "That's Mom." He folded a piece of bacon into his mouth. "When were you thinking of doing it—putting the camera up there?"

"Right away, now," Xander said. "I don't know how long it'll take to set up, and I definitely want it working before we go to bed, in case whatever went on last night goes on again."

"The hardware store's on the other side of town," Toria said.

She had gone there with Dad the other day to get locks for the third-floor doors—locks the house had shaken off the way a dog shakes off fleas.

"That's a long ride," David said.

Xander's bike was a secondhand three-speed with a loose chain and a wobbly wheel.

"I'll take the car again." Seeing David's frown, he said, "If the cops see me, it doesn't matter whether I'm walking or riding my bike or chasing poodles up Main Street in a Ferrari—they're going to haul me away."

David considered telling Xander that getting a camera wasn't worth leaving the house. It wasn't worth risking being spotted by the police. Then he realized how much time it would take to buy it and then install it . . . time *not* spent finding the Civil War world. As much as David wanted to find Mom, he *didn't* want Toria going over. By the time the camera was ready, and his brother started thinking again about sending their sister over, maybe Dad would be home to nix Xander's stupid plan.

David looked at his brother out of the corner of his eye. He said, "I would feel a lot safer knowing what's happening up there."

Xander nodded. "I'll go in a few minutes." He snapped up a slice of toast, folded it, and stuffed it into his mouth. Chewing while he talked, he said, "Toria, you look for the Civil War world while I'm gone. If you find it, stay in the antechamber. That'll keep it from shifting away."

David pulled in a breath, sucking egg down the wrong pipe. He started to choke and let food fall from his mouth onto the plate, not caring what it looked like. Xander stood and slapped him on the back, hard. Then again. Whatever was in there cleared. David swallowed and breathed.

Toria ran around the table to rub his back. "Are you all right?" she said sweetly.

He nodded, cleared his throat. His eyes had begun to water, and he wiped them. He took a swig of juice.

Xander dropped back into his seat and watched David with big eyes. He said, "Wouldn't it be a trip if you choked to death on eggs, after all the things you've survived lately?"

David glared at him. "It would be *sad,*" he said, his voice hoarse.

"For us," Xander said. "You wouldn't care. You'd be gone."

David couldn't help but smile. He said, "I'd care. Just before the lights went out for good, I'd be thinking *Eggs? Eggs? You gotta be kidding!*"

Even Toria laughed. The sound of it reminded David why he'd choked in the first place. He said, "Xander, we can't look for the world while you're gone. It's too dangerous."

Xander frowned. He said, "We should get Mom first, then. That's the most important thing."

"It is," David said. "But what if it takes a while for the world to come back around? What if something keeps Toria from getting Mom? Then we'll be back in bed tonight, wondering what's happening on the third floor. Let's just get that done and be covered."

Toria was still standing next to David, pressing into his arm.

He said, "Toria, I'm all right. Go finish eating."

"I'm not hungry anymore." She was scrunching her nose, looking at the food that had fallen from David's mouth.

David covered the mess with a slice of toast. He said, "Just go sit down, okay?"

"Yeah," Xander said. "I think we can get a camera system up and running pretty fast. Let's do that, then we'll look for the Civil War stuff."

"Too bad we can't put a camera in all the rooms up there . . . in all the *antechambers,*" Toria said, leaning back in her chair.

David smiled. He could tell she was still trying to get a handle on that word *antechamber.* He wasn't sure if *he'd* ever heard it before coming here. Now they used it like a thousand times a day. He felt his smile fade. He wished he didn't know it, that they'd never discovered that stupid third floor.

Xander's eyes grew wide, his lips made a perfect O. He said, "Then we could see which items are in the antechambers anytime we wanted to."

David said, "It'd take a week to set up twenty cameras like that."

"But wouldn't that be cool?"

"It'd be cooler," David said, "not to *need* the cameras. Let's get Mom and get gone."

Xander pushed his lips sideways. "I'll just get one extra camera to see if it even works in an antechamber."

"I wish Dad was here," Toria said.

"They took him at about seven thirty last night," Xander said. He wiggled his fingers, calculating. "That's fifteen hours ago. He said he thought it was all a scam, that they didn't dare hold him longer than a day."

"That's nine more hours," David said. He was more than a little upset that the house had made a few hours seem like an eternity, like they were holding on to the ledge of a cliff and their fingers were growing tired. He wished everything would just slow down so they could take a breath, so they could *think.*

"After I put the camera up, we'll go get Mom," Xander told Toria. "If you're still up for it."

David hoped she would drop her face, say something like, *I changed my mind. I'm too scared.*

But she didn't. She puffed out her chest and said, "I can do it!"

"Okay," Xander said. He lifted his glass of juice. "To being strong and courageous."

Toria and David picked up their own glasses and clinked them against Xander's.

Despite his feelings about Toria going over, David joined them. "Strong and courageous!" he said.

CHAPTER

twenty-six

WEDNESDAY, NOON

David sat in the Mission Control Center, his head bowed toward the PSP in his hands. His teeth pushed into his bottom lip as he clicked the buttons that caused his on-screen soccer player to make a bicycle kick for the goal: right past the tender and in! As the crowd roared and a teammate gave him a high five, he glanced up to a computer monitor on a desk in front of him.

Xander's face filled the screen. The camera he'd picked up at the hardware store after breakfast made his eyes appear unnaturally large. The pencil he held in his mouth looked more like a horse's bit. He was squinting over the camera, so it seemed like he was staring at David's hair. Xander looked over his shoulder at the crooked hallway of doors behind him, then wiggled the camera around. He was mounting it above the doorway between the third-floor landing and the hall.

Static flashed on the screen, then a band of snow scrolled from the top of the screen to the bottom.

"We're getting interference!" David called over his shoulder.

"What?" Toria called back from the base of the stairs leading to the third floor. She was roughly midway between David and Xander and was conveying their words back and forth.

"We're getting—" David started.

More static broke Xander's face across the screen.

"Hold on!" David said. He pushed back from the desk and stepped out of the MCC.

They had turned what Mom had called the servants' quarters into their base of operations for her rescue. The room was off a short hallway that jutted back toward the rear of the house from the second floor's main hallway. It was close to the staircase leading to the third level, where twenty doors led into twenty small rooms and, beyond them, twenty portals opened into different times, different "worlds"—all of them on earth, but so unlike the time and places the Kings knew, they might as well have been alien planets.

The staircase itself was hidden behind the wall at the end of the short hallway. One evening David and Xander had spotted the big man—the one Xander dubbed Phemus—in their house. They'd followed him and found a secret door in the wall.

Now, David stepped into the opening of that door. Six feet beyond it was another wall, this one coated in unpainted plaster. Even the unsanded swirls of the trowel that had applied the plaster were still visible. Whoever had built it wasn't concerned about appearances: the wall was nothing more than a barrier to keep people out. Or more likely, David thought, to keep people *in*, to keep them from coming through the portals and into the main part of the house, as Phemus had done when he took Mom. Set in this second wall—not directly in front of the secret door, but off to the side—was another door, covered in metal.

Lot of good the extra security did, David thought.

The metal door was open, and Toria was leaning against its frame.

"What?" she said.

"Just looking," David said.

"What's going on?" Xander called from the floor above.

"We're getting static," David yelled. "I'm wondering if there's anything between the camera and the monitor that's causing it."

He scanned the area between the walls, about the size of a walk-in closet. The backside of the hallway wall was imperfectly finished, like the other one.

David stepped past Toria to the base of the steps that rose straight up to the landing. He could hear Xander fiddling with something, but his brother was out of sight, in the hallway to the left of the landing. He rapped his knuckles against this second wall, but the sound told him nothing about what was inside.

"I can't tell," he said. "There might be wires running through the walls that are interfering."

"Get back to the monitor," Xander said. "I'll fiddle with the camera, see what I can do."

"Get back to the monitor!" Toria yelled into David's ear, trying to be funny. They had told her to yell to the other whatever one of them said. "I'll fiddle—!"

David clamped his hand over her mouth. "I heard," he said. He wiggled a fingertip into his ear, frowning at her. "That hurt."

He went through the secret door into the short hall and returned to the MCC. The room was coming along. Dad had hung a timeline of history near the ceiling; it spanned the length of two walls. Tough guys from Xander's movie posters—*300, Gladiator, Remember the Titans*—stared down at him. They were meant to psych them up to face the dangers of the other worlds. A series of colored index cards was taped to the wall, reflecting the times and places they'd already visited: the Roman Colosseum, the tiger-and-warrior-infested jungle, the French village during World War II, the Civil War, the peaceful world where Dad and Xander had first carved Bob into a tree. David still wanted to add cards that listed the items they had found in the antechambers and link the cards with string. He wondered if he'd ever find the time to do that.

He dropped into the chair in front of the monitor. On the screen, a brief pop of static fluttered across Xander's face. His brother's mouth moved.

"How's that?" Toria yelled.

Now that David knew what Xander had said, he recognized the way his mouth had moved to form the words. If they did this long enough, he might learn to read lips. That'd be sweet.

"Better!" he hollered back to Toria. "But tell him to move it a little to the left!"

She passed it along, and Xander nudged the camera angle the wrong way.

"*My* left! The camera's left!" David yelled. He heard his sister echo the words.

Xander rolled his eyes. He adjusted the camera, raised his eyebrows in question.

"That's good!" David said.

Xander nodded, took the pencil out of his mouth, and made a mark off camera. His head filled the monitor, then it dropped away. The camera was turned sideways, pointing down the hall. David realized Xander had set it on top of the stepladder while he went to get the screws and screwdriver. Xander moved away from the camera and squatted in front of a box.

David picked up the PSP. The game was over, his team's score in the toilet. He turned it off. He'd rather be kicking his ball around outside than doing this.

Xander walked toward the monitor, screws in one hand, the tool in the other. The camera jerked and bounced around, then settled on the image David had seen a minute before: the hallway of doors over Xander's shoulder.

Xander said something. In the few seconds before Toria could relay it, David tried to guess what it was: *Is the dog dead? I'm a raft? Want to fight?*

"Is that right?" Toria yelled.

Oooo . . . not even close.

"Yeah, perfect!" he said.

Xander moved a screw to the mount behind the camera. The screwdriver came into view, then disappeared from the frame.

David smiled at the faces Xander was making as he tried to get the screw into the wall. Xander's tongue appeared in the corner of his mouth, and David outright laughed. He yelled, "Ha-ha-ha!"

"What?" Toria called.

"Pass it along," David said. "Ha-ha-ha!"

He heard her call out to Xander. On the monitor, Xander's eyebrows came together. He moved his mouth, a word David could read: *What?* Toria repeated it. On the monitor, Xander said something else—too long for David even to guess at.

Toria yelled, "He said knock it off or you can put the camera up."

Xander looked down, probably getting another screw. Then his brother was back to twisting his hand over the screwdriver and making funny faces.

David snickered. A burst of static obscured Xander's face, then scattered away. As it did, David's heart turned to stone. He leaned forward and grabbed the side edges of the monitor.

Over Xander's shoulder, the camera showed the hallway running back to the far wall, which had been, until seconds ago, cloaked in shadows. Now light filled that space. Though David could not see it, he knew only one thing could have caused such brightness: way back at the end of the hall, a door had opened. The light flickered, as though something was moving through it, casting a shadow.

The big man stepped into the hallway.

Phemus!

His bald head almost scraped the ceiling. Wiry hair burst from his face and hung down to his powerful chest. Even in the camera's poor resolution, David could make out the scars that crisscrossed his flesh, the smudges of dirt, the glistening sweat. A raggedy pelt hung from his waist. The man swung his head around to squint back into the light, as though debating about pulling the door closed.

David jumped up, sending his chair clattering to the floor behind him. "Xander!" he screamed. He spun, intending to bolt out of the room, but the corner of his eye caught something on the monitor, and he turned back.

The big man reversed a step as *another* man came out of the room. This one was similar to Phemus: a little smaller—still large—with a full head of long, shaggy hair. He peered into Phemus's face as if for instructions.

"Xan—Xander!" David yelled. He stumbled backward, pivoted around, and crashed into Toria, who was running into the room. They both went down. David's cast cracked against the floor beside his sister's head, sending a bolt of pain shooting into his shoulder and neck.

"David!" Toria grunted under him, pushing him off.

David scrambled to get his feet under him. He screamed, "Xander! Get out of there! Xander!"

As he rose, Toria pushed herself into a sitting position. "What are you—" she said, then let loose with her own piercing scream.

She was looking at the monitor. David snapped his head toward it. A third man had emerged from the room. Like the others, he wore only a tattered pelt. But he was shorter, and so skinny his ribs pushed through his skin. He had splotchy hair springing out from his scalp like water from a colander.

He bounced up and down, looking from Phemus to the other man like a pet hungry for attention.

Toria wrapped both of her arms around David's leg. He yanked on it, but her grip was a bear trap.

"Toria, let go!"

On the monitor, Xander was still making faces, cranking on the screwdriver.

"Turn around, Xander!" David screamed. *Can't you hear them! Why can't you hear them?*

He wondered if the house was messing with the sounds, intentionally keeping Xander from hearing the people behind him.

His brother plucked a screw from his lips and brought his hand past the camera's lens. Over his shoulder, the three men turned their heads. They spotted Xander and began lumbering toward him.

CHAPTER twenty-seven

Wednesday, 12:06 p.m.

David turned, twisting his leg free from Toria's grasp. He stumbled into the hall and darted for the secret door. It was closed. He slammed against the wall beside it. He tapped the edge of the door with his fingers, but it didn't pop out as it usually did.

"They're getting closer!" Toria yelled from the MCC. She ran up behind him. "Hurry, Dae!"

"I am!" He pounded on the door. It wouldn't budge. "Why'd you close it?"

"I didn't!"

This house!

He looked around, didn't see anything he could use to pry open the door or break it down. Then he remembered and ran into the MCC. Propped against the wall, just inside the door, was the toy rifle both he and Xander had used as a club. He snatched it up.

Frantic as he was to get to Xander, he just *had to* glance at the monitor. His brother was still squinting past the lens, messing with screws and the screwdriver. Behind him, the two larger men were trudging shoulder to shoulder toward him. The smaller, animal-like man was hopping up and down behind them, his eyes wild. In a flash, he tried to squeeze between one of the other men and the wall, but the space was too tight. They had crossed half the distance to Xander.

David sprinted into the hallway. Toria was beating her fists against the secret door.

"Move!" David said. He swung the gun's stock into the wall, blasting a divot of wallpaper and plaster from it. "Xander!"

He didn't have time to tear down the whole wall, but he definitely had the energy and determination. He stepped back and rammed the barrel of the rifle into the wall near the latch. The muzzle made a half-inch-deep hole. He had hit a wooden stud.

He pulled back, rammed again. This time the barrel plunged through up to the trigger. David began rotating the stock with both hands as though turning a handle on a butter churn.

The hole in the wall opened up around the barrel. Plaster fell away. When the opening was the diameter of a dinner plate, he pushed the rifle all the way through. It clattered to the floor on the other side.

If this doesn't work, Xander's dead.

David reached his hand through and found the latch. It wouldn't budge. Maybe his pounding had jammed it.

He pulled his arm out and stuck his face to the hole. "Xander!"

"What?"

"Run! Look behind you!"

"What are you—" Then he screamed, a sound that pierced David's heart like a spear.

Metal rattled and crashed. David realized the ladder had fallen.

"Xander!"

David felt the latch again. He forced himself to slow down, to feel it and picture it. He realized that the lever was pushed too far forward. He pulled it backward, then tugged it down. The wall sprang open. He hooked his fingers around it and pulled.

"Toria," he said, "make sure this door doesn't shut again."

His brother's screams continued. David ran through the

second doorway and pounded up the stairs. He hit the landing and spun into the hallway.

Xander was ten feet in, blood smeared across his forehead. Phemus clutched his ankle and was dragging him down the hall. The other two men lurched in to grab at him. But Xander had hold of the aluminum stepladder and was wielding it the way a lion tamer uses a chair to hold back the man-eaters. He was flat on his back, hefting the ladder up, shoving the top of it at his attackers.

David ran forward. He grabbed the ladder and pulled. "Xander, let go! I've got better leverage than you!"

"David!" Xander released his grip.

David pulled the ladder back, yelled—because he had to say something, had to release the knot of thoughts pressuring his brain—"Let go of my brother!" and jammed the ladder's top brace into Phemus's face.

Blood sprayed out of the man's nose. He stumbled back, an expression of complete shock on his face.

"Ha!" David screamed, as though he'd scored the winning point in a video game.

The smaller, spastic intruder—David's frenzied mind instantly tagged this guy "Baboon Man"—stretched to grab the leg Phemus had lost.

Xander kicked the hand. It pulled away, then reached out again. Another kick. The hand retreated, reached again.

David reared back with the ladder and heaved it forward

with every bit of energy he had in him. It struck Baboon Man in the side of the skull with a loud *crack!* The man's head snapped sideways, and he reeled away.

The other two—Phemus, bloody from David's first strike, and the one who was almost as large—lunged for Xander.

Xander bent his knees, placed the treads of his sneakers on the carpet, and pushed himself backward, toward the landing.

David jabbed the ladder at the men. It struck Phemus's chest. David may as well have rammed it into a brick wall: the man didn't budge. The shock of hitting him reverberated along the ladder and through David's bones. His broken arm throbbed.

Xander pushed past him on the floor.

"Go!" David yelled. "Go!"

Xander flipped over and clambered on his hands and knees toward the landing. He yelled, "I'm clear, Dae! Get out of there."

David lunged with the ladder.

This time he caught Baboon Man in the chest. The man *oophed!* and stumbled back again.

Phemus grabbed the ladder and ripped it out of David's hands. He flung it into the wall, smashing one of the wall lamps. David witnessed the briefest flash of satisfaction on the man's scruffy face.

David spun and darted for Xander, who was pulling himself up against the door frame. The brothers collided. Their legs tangled, and they fell onto the landing.

The men in the hallway lurched forward, their arms outstretched. It occurred to David that Xander would already have a zombie movie in mind to describe this later—if there *was* a later. David flung himself down the stairs, bringing Xander with him. They tumbled over the first steps, grunting, groaning. Then David found himself going down backwards, his butt bouncing painfully against each step. He raised his cast for balance, and Xander's forehead flew into it. They both yelped in pain. They reached the bottom, and Xander flipped over David, crashing into the wall.

Above them, the men pushed through the doorway, their eyes huge and insane.

David scrambled up, and he saw Phemus take the lead, lumbering slowly down each step. His girth spanned the width of the stairwell. Baboon Man leaped and pulled himself up behind Phemus as though he were scaling a wall. His fingers were bent talons, digging into the big man's flesh at the shoulders and on top of his head, trying to propel himself over.

Xander grabbed David's collar and yanked him through the doorway. Both brothers grabbed for the door at the same time. Swinging the door around, they tripped over each other. Only their iron grips on the door's edge kept them from spilling to the floor.

Through the opening, David saw that Baboon Man—scrawny, scraggly, jittery—had gotten himself completely onto Phemus's shoulder. For a moment he was perched there, squatting like a gargoyle, his wicked grin trembling over his knees. Then he leaped off, a screeching beast of prey. Arms outstretched, mouth impossibly wide, he flew at David.

The door slammed shut. The impact behind it knocked it open again, flinging David into the wall behind him. Air burst out of his lungs. He inhaled, got nothing, inhaled. He slid down the wall.

Xander was pushing on the door, but Baboon Man had collapsed onto the floor, halfway through. He wasn't moving. Just out cold.

David gasped for breath that wouldn't come.

Xander grabbed him. "It's okay, Dae. Just got the wind knocked out of you. It'll come back." He hoisted him up. "Toria!" he called. "Help Dae. Get him out of here."

David felt Toria's small hands hook themselves into his armpits from behind. It was just enough support to keep him on his feet, and he started backpedaling through the secret door. He watched Xander try to push the unconscious Baboon Man out of the way of the door.

The guy groaned, lifted his head, tried to push himself up.

Xander kicked him in the head.

Baboon Man's hand shot out and seized Xander's ankle.

"Wait," David wheezed at Toria. "Let go. I'm okay." He pulled free, stooped, and picked up the toy rifle.

Something crashed into the other side of the wall—David

imagined Phemus picking up speed on the stairs and nailing the wall with arms the size of battering rams. Plaster dust filled the small space between the walls as the entire wall at the base of the stairs broke free from the ceiling and fell.

CHAPTER

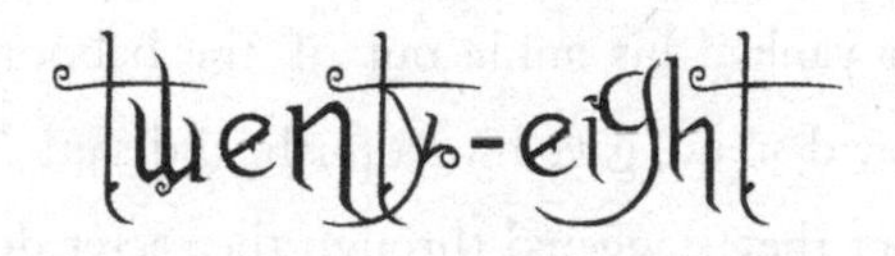

WEDNESDAY, 12:14 P.M.

The wall tipped over, striking David's head. He crumpled onto his hands and knees. The wall slammed into the hall-way wall, angling from the floor like the side of a pup tent.

Xander had ducked, avoiding the wall by inches. Baboon Man squirmed on the ground toward Xander, whose ankle he continued to clasp with that bony, taloned hand. David hammered the rifle butt into the man's skull.

The guy twisted his face toward David. He growled like

a dog and snapped his mouth open and closed. David gave the guy's forehead a quick, hard jab. His head dropped to the floor.

The wall suffered another devastating blow from the staircase side. Chunks of plaster fell—one giving David another firm knock on the head.

"Xander," he said, "we have to get out of here. The whole wall's coming down."

Dust stung his eyes, filled his already aching lungs. He coughed.

Xander yanked his ankle out of the baboon's claw. He helped David stand, gave him a push, and said, "Go!"

Together they staggered through the secret door into the second-floor hallway.

"Toria, shut the door," David said, panting. "It's not going to stop them, but still . . ." He rubbed his head where the wall and the plaster had hit it. Between his arm, his head, and his bruised backside, he felt like he had just climbed out of a clothes dryer.

Toria swung the door shut, and the latch clicked.

A crash came from the other side, and this outer wall, decorated to look like any other in the hallway, buckled toward them. It cracked from floor to ceiling, and the secret door popped open.

Toria screamed. David grabbed her shoulder, Xander grabbed David's, and they backpedaled past the MCC.

"What are they doing?" David said.

Xander said, "When the wall collapsed, it made the door opening too small for Phemus to fit through. Now he has to come *through* the walls."

"What do we do?" Toria said.

Before they could answer, an explosion erupted at the end of the short hallway. The entire wall fell forward, creaking and cracking. Sparks flashed as electrical wiring broke. The lights went out. Sunlight from the foyer and the open MCC door revealed the wall crashing to the floor, followed by the second wall; it landed on top of the first one. A massive dust cloud billowed up, as though a giant hand had slapped a pile of baby powder. It roiled in the hallway, coming at them like a sandstorm.

Xander said, "Run!"

He grabbed Toria's hand, and they ran around the corner into the second floor's main hallway.

David's legs froze. He watched as a figure stirred in the dust cloud. It became more distinct, solidifying into arms, legs, a head. To the left of this silhouette, the other big man stepped out of the haze. He was grinning and taking long, crunching strides toward him.

David's legs broke from the invisible cement that had bound them, and he ran. He called out, "The closet!"

Xander and Toria skidded to a stop at the head of the grand staircase.

"School's in session," Xander said. "We can't—"

"Yes, we can!" David said. "Two of those guys are too big to fit in the locker. The other might be out cold. Who cares if people wonder where we came from?"

The two men trudged around the corner.

Toria screamed, pulled her hand out of Xander's, and bolted down the stairs.

"Wait!" David said. "Toria!"

Xander grabbed for her, but her legs were moving like a race car's pistons; she was almost to the bottom before he took a single step. The brothers threw panicked glances at each other and tore after her.

Toria reached the front door and yanked on it. It didn't open.

David pushed ahead, thumbed the dead bolt, and opened the door. He grabbed his sister's wrist and flung her through the opening. She leaped off the porch. Xander turned in the doorway, and both boys looked up to the top of the stairs.

The hulking men glowered down at them. Their chests rose and fell. Their eyes, dark under heavy brows, blinked, blinked, as though they were unaccustomed to the bright sunlight.

Xander stepped forward into the foyer.

David touched his arm. "Xander?" he whispered.

His brother straightened his spine, squared his shoulders. "You!" he said, pointing at Phemus.

David remembered what Xander had said about the poster he'd seen: Odysseus challenging the Cyclops.

Xander said, "Where's our mother? Bring her back! Just . . ." His voice cracked. His breathing was fast and shallow. His next words were menacingly quiet. "Bring her back."

David was afraid his brother was going to rush the guy. The last time they'd met, when the man had kidnapped Mom, all three of the King men—Dad, Xander, and David—had almost died. And Xander had been armed with a metal bat. No way the outcome of a confrontation now could be any better. In fact, David was sure it would end up much worse.

He stepped closer and shifted the toy rifle to his left hand. He clasped the fingers of his right hand into Xander's waistband. "Xander, let's go," he said. "Come on. This isn't a fair fight. It's not meant to be. We're supposed to lose."

"We're not going to leave," Xander told the man. His words sounded hard as rocks. "We're staying until our mother's back." He started to turn, then said, "The next time I see you, I'll be ready."

Without taking his eyes off Xander, Phemus began descending the stairs. The wood under his bare feet creaked in protest. The other man grinned and trailed a step behind.

"Xander!" David said. He tugged his brother's pants, yanking him back—a step, then two, till they were on the porch. Toria stood in the woods, watching them.

Xander frowned at David. His eyes were red.

As David watched, a thick rivulet of blood from a cut above Xander's eye ran the curve of his brow, skirted the corner of his eye, and ran down his cheek. It would have made a great movie-tough-guy wound.

They looked through the open door. Here in the sunlight, the interior looked dark and gloomy. The sound of the men's plodding footsteps echoed out to them.

Xander gestured with his head. He whispered, "Let's go."

CHAPTER

twenty-nine

WEDNESDAY, 12:20 P.M.

David and Xander descended the porch steps. When they reached Toria in the woods, they turned back.

"Think they'll come out for us?" David said.

Xander shook his head. "That house is their leash. It's as far as their master will let them go."

"Taksidian?" David said. He had heard Taksidian talking to Phemus the other day, when Clayton had chased David through the locker into the house.

"Who else?" Xander said. He still looked ready to rumble.

David thought it would be a short brawl if he and the big guy ever did tangle. He pointed at the blood on Xander's face. "What happened?"

Xander touched the cut and grimaced. He looked at his fingers. "The ladder," he said. "When those guys pulled me off, it came down on my head."

The shadows inside the doorway stirred. Phemus filled the opening. He scowled out at the daylight, caught sight of the kids, and glared at them.

"Are you sure about the leash?" Toria said.

"Yeah," Xander said. "I'm starting to figure things—"

The brute stepped onto the porch.

Toria grabbed David's bicep. David gripped Xander's shirt.

"It's okay," Xander said. "That's it. That's as far as he'll come."

The man lumbered to the porch steps and started down.

Toria gasped.

"Ow, Toria," David whispered. "Your nails are digging into my skin."

"Get ready to run," Xander said.

"Where to?" David said.

"Follow me. I have an idea."

David nudged Toria. "You hear? Follow Xander. Don't run off like you did down the stairs."

"I got scared," she said.

"No kidding."

They watched the man reach the dirt at the bottom of the steps. He turned back to his . . . *friend* was the word that came to David's mind, but it was a little like thinking of two killer Rottweilers as play-date pals.

"Let's get out of here," Xander said, and took off.

David grabbed Toria's wrist and fell in behind. He looked back over his shoulder to see Phemus swing his arm in a *Come on!* gesture, but the smaller man backed away and disappeared in the gloom. It took Phemus all of three seconds to spot the kids and start after them.

Xander weaved through the trees and bushes, arcing around the side of the house.

The man's feet pounded the ground behind them, snapping twigs and ripping through the low bushes and rotting deadfalls the kids had jumped over.

"He's getting closer," Toria said.

Xander picked up his pace. He said, "I didn't think that guy could move so fast."

"Like you didn't think he could leave the house," David said.

"All right, all right." Xander angled around a thick bush.

"Anything else you think he *can't* do," David said, "so I have a heads-up about what he's *going* to do?"

"We're about to find out," Xander said.

They broke through a thick patch of bushes and stopped in the clearing. It was an oval-shaped meadow about half the size of a football field. Encircled by trees, the ground here was flat and uniformly covered with lush, green grass. The upper branches of the trees bent inward, hanging over the meadow's edges. The sky above was blue and streaked with clouds, as though brushed with white paint.

David and Xander had discovered the place on their second day in the house. Here, the air was peculiar, and their voices became squeaky, as though they were auditioning for the part of Mickey Mouse in a movie. They could also run faster and jump higher.

But Dad had shown them the clearing's real magic: here, they could *fly*. That was the best word David could think of. What else could you call rising above the ground and moving through the air without wings, wires, or equipment of any kind? But it wasn't just a question of taking off, the way birds fly. You had to find currents, like air currents, but they weren't windy. Then you had to step on them, ride them.

Uh-oh, David thought. He whispered, "Xander, Toria can't do it. Remember?"

Xander had forgotten. He said, "Not at all? Toria?"

She gazed at the grass, shook her head.

"No, no," Xander said. "That's okay." His head snapped up. "Shhh."

The sound of clomping feet grew louder.

Xander waved the others closer. He said, "Toria, try." He looked David in the eyes. "David," he said, "*fly*."

CHAPTER

Wednesday, 12:32 p.m.

David dropped the toy rifle. He held his hands open to the ground as though he were mounting a skateboard. He lifted his foot and felt the air with it. Nothing. He moved deeper into the clearing.

Outside the ring of trees and heavy bushes, something crashed.

David's heart revved up. If he couldn't do it . . . if Toria couldn't . . . there was nowhere to hide. They would have to fight the man, which to David's perspective was like taking on Godzilla.

He felt the air with his foot again: searching for an invisible platform. He remembered thinking that Dad's ability to ride the clearing's currents was like standing on an escalator no one could see. With that image in mind, he raised his foot and tried to *stand* on the air. His foot stomped the ground. He tried again. No go. He sighed and looked over at Xander.

His brother was hovering four feet over the grass. His feet slipped one way and then the other. He zipped higher. He smiled; David remembered the clearing had a way of making them giddy and carefree. But they didn't dare laugh now, not with Phemus tromping around so near.

David swung his foot over the grass. Something snagged his ankle. His foot rose. When it reached the height of his chest, his other foot came off the ground as well. He pinwheeled his arms and fell backward. He closed his eyes and pulled his cast in close to his chest, bracing himself for a crash. The impact never came.

He opened his eyes, turned his head. He was flat on his back, five feet off the ground. Using his stomach muscles, he forced his upper body into a vertical inclination. Now he was sitting—and more than fifteen feet in the air. He was drifting, rising like a balloon. He started moving his arms and legs as he would have in water. He shot forward, arched up, spiraled down.

Xander's waving caught his attention. His brother touched his finger to his lips and pointed at Toria. She was hopping up and down, stepping on currents that weren't there and generally throwing a quiet fit. The boys swam to her, converging above her shoulders.

"Toria," Xander whispered.

She snapped her face up, startled to find her brothers hovering directly above her.

"Give us your hands," David said.

She hesitated.

Xander said, "We won't drop you."

The bushes rustled nearby.

Toria raised her arms and closed her eyes.

David gripped her wrist in both of his hands and squeezed.

"Not so hard," she whispered.

He let up, but only a little. The image of his sister falling four stories tightened his stomach and made him want to clamp down even harder.

Xander got his hands around her wrists. They raised their heads, bringing their feet down, and kicked. Nothing happened. They kicked again and drifted up a few inches. Again—and another few inches.

"We have to do better," Xander said. "He'll see us if we take too long."

David nodded and closed his eyes. He imagined lifting his dad's barbells. He kicked and kicked, mentally bringing those barbells up from the bottom of a pool. Kick. Kick.

An insect fluttered onto the top of his head. He jerked his head sideways, but it wouldn't go away.

Better not be a spider, he thought.

"David," Xander whispered.

"I'm trying." Their voices were high-pitched, but either because he was so frightened or he was getting used to it, David hardly noticed.

"Open your eyes."

When he did, leaves hung down around Xander's head. A branch curled behind him, like the backdrop of a school photograph.

David tilted his head. What he had thought was an insect was the forest's canopy, leaning over the edge of the meadow. He looked down. Toria dangled between them. And *way* below her sneakered feet was the ground. It was scary for *him,* and he could fly.

He told Toria, "Don't look down."

Of course she did. She began wiggling around. Her movements jerked David down, up, down, up, like a fishing bobber.

"Toria," David whispered. "Stop it."

She whined.

"You're not making this easy," he said.

She swung her head back to look at David. Her blue eyes

danced in their sockets, reflecting the frightened pace of her heart.

David whispered, "You've got Dad's eyes, you know. So does Xander."

The randomness of his statement caught her off guard, distracting her from her panic just a little bit. She blinked at him, then adjusted her vision to Xander.

Xander smiled. "Guess we better give them back."

Her lips didn't so much as smile as they did not frown.

"Hey," David whispered, "have you heard this one? Birdie, birdie, in the sky, why'd you do that in my eye? Boy, I'm glad that cows don't fly."

Toria started to chuckle, caught herself, and bit her lip. Her feet slowly stopped their midair pedaling.

Below them, Phemus plowed through the bushes and then stumbled into the clearing.

CHAPTER thirty-one

WEDNESDAY, 12:39 P.M.

Leaves and twigs fell off the big man's shoulders. He swiveled his head around, clearly surprised to have lost his prey. From their perspective of almost directly above him, the man didn't look as huge as David knew he was. All he could see were his gleaming dome, planklike shoulders, swinging arms.

Toria took in her brothers' worried expressions and started to bring her gaze down.

David stopped her. "Hey," he said, quieter than a whisper. He shook his head. "Don't."

"I'll be all right," she mouthed, without making a sound.

When she looked, David felt her arm muscles tighten up. She turned her face back to him.

"It's okay," David said.

"Dae," Xander said. "Let's stay directly over him."

David nodded. It was the least likely place the guy would look. Even if he glanced up, the chances of his looking *straight* up were pretty slim.

Especially with that fat neck of his, David thought.

He wasn't about to release his hand from Toria's wrist, so the only way to adjust their position in relation to the man below was to wiggle and kick. It reminded David of people in movies who have their feet and arms tied; mimicking a snake or caterpillar, they somehow managed to escape.

The man spotted something. He walked to it and picked it up: the toy rifle.

David and Xander wiggled and kicked until they were once again directly over his head. If they dropped Toria, David thought, she would land right on the guy. No doubt it would hurt Toria a lot more than it would the brute. David closed his eyes and tightened his grip on her wrists.

"Ow," she whispered. When he peeked, she mouthed, "Not so tight!"

Below her, the man turned in a circle. He examined the toy as though it might tell him where they'd gone. He headed toward the center of the clearing.

The boys kicked and wiggled to stay with him, but he walked too fast. David cast a concerned look at Xander.

Xander stopped wiggling. He whispered, "Toria, grab my wrist. Good. Now grab Dae's."

When she did, they were not only holding her, but she was also holding them.

Xander said, "Trust me?"

The concern etched into her features deepened.

No kidding, David thought. *That's like the last thing I'd want to hear in her position.*

Still, she nodded.

Xander released his right hand. Toria's eyes flashed wide, then she realized their mutual grip was strong and she gave him a little smile. Xander nodded at David, who released his left hand from her wrist.

They used their free hands to paddle through the air. They could move much more quickly and accurately. Again, they stopped directly above the man.

Toria kept her eyes turned up. She looked from brother to brother, at the canopy of leaves around their heads . . . anywhere but down. Then she squinted at Xander, a puzzled expression forming on her face. "Xan—"

Something small fell away from him. Toria squeezed her

eyes closed. It struck her forehead: a bright red splatter that took the shape of a starburst.

Blood.

The cut above Xander's brow was oozing again. At the edge of the wound, a droplet swelled like a tiny balloon. David's eyes grew with it.

Xander realized what had landed on his sister and began swinging his hand around to the cut—too late: another droplet fell. It missed hitting Toria by less than an inch.

It was so small, by the time it passed her sneakers David had lost sight of it. He held his breath, hoping he had miscalculated the drop's trajectory.

But he hadn't: a small dot appeared on the crown of the man's head.

Phemus raised his hand and rubbed the spot. Then he examined his palm. He looked straight up and grinned.

CHAPTER thirty-two

WEDNESDAY, 12:45 P.M.

Staring down at Phemus's upturned face, Toria screamed.

"Shhh," Xander said. "He's down there, we're up here. He can't do anything."

"Well, that means he can," David said.

"Shhh," Xander repeated.

Continuing to watch them, Phemus backed away.

"Do we follow him?" David asked.

"No point now," Xander said.

Phemus bent his right arm way behind his back.

"What's he—"

"Oh, no," David said. "Move! Move!" He began kicking and wiggling and paddling with his left hand.

Phemus hurled the toy rifle at them. It spun round and round like a circular saw. David heard it cutting through the air like the blades of a helicopter: *whoop-whoop-whoop.* It was heading for Toria.

"Pull her, Xander," David said. "Pull!"

They tugged, raising her between them six inches, twelve inches. The rifle smacked into her ankle. It struck so hard, her legs swung out from under her.

Toria threw her head back and screamed. Her eyes were pinched shut, but her tears found their way out, pooling against her lids and the bridge of her nose. She cried—horrible, wrenching sobs.

David couldn't stand it, watching his little sister cry in pain, unable to do anything about it. They couldn't even check her ankle, rub it, do anything to make it feel better.

"Toria," David said. "I'm sorry."

He felt as though her pain was his. He had never experienced this so clearly: not when Phemus had knocked out Dad or when he had sent Xander crashing into the wall while kidnapping Mom or when the lock blew off one of the doors, gouging Dad's hand.

He said, "We'll get out of this, Tor. We will."

She nodded. She straightened her head, so she was looking neither up nor down, and wept quietly. That pulled on David's heart even more than her wailing agony had done. It was like her *spirit* hurt.

David focused on Phemus's movements, and his stomach took a tumble all over again. The big man was approaching the toy rifle. After hitting his sister, it had spun down, landing at the edge of the clearing. Phemus stooped, snatched it up, then squinted at the three King children.

"We have to do something," David said.

"For one thing," Xander said, "let's protect Toria better."

"How?"

"Pull her up between us," Xander said. "If she puts her arms around our shoulders, and we reach across her back and under her arms, she'll be sandwiched between us. We'll get hit before she does."

"That's okay with me," David said. He tried not to think about what that meant, but images came anyway: the barrel of the gun tearing into his side, the stock cracking into his skull.

"Toria," Xander said, "we'll raise you, and you have to climb up our bodies. Get your arms around our shoulders, okay?"

Her eyes followed the path she would take. "But that means letting go of your arms. I can't do that!"

"Try," David said. "Toria, you'll be safer up here with us."

"Move!" Xander yelled.

David caught a glimpse of the rifle spinning toward them. Both he and Xander threw themselves backward. *Whoop-whoop-whoop.* The weapon sailed over their arched chests, right where their heads had been seconds earlier. It sliced into the forest's canopy, then plunged to the meadow.

David and Xander pulled Toria as high as they could. She released her grip on David's arm and quickly grabbed his shoulder, then did the same with Xander. Their heads were nearly touching, their arms wrapped around each other.

Xander surveyed their surroundings. "How about we—*whoa!*"

Whoop-whoop-whoop!

The rifle sailed up. Xander reached out to grab it. There was a *clack-clack* sound, as though he'd stuck his hand into a fan. He yelled and pulled his arm back. David saw a gash running across the back of his hand.

Once again Phemus plucked the weapon off the ground.

David said, "Whatever we're going to do, we better do it now."

Xander drifted into a beam of sunlight. He blinked, turned his face toward it. "Okay, okay, I got it," he said.

Phemus circled below them, hefting the rifle like a ball-player about to throw a pitch.

"*Now,* Xander!" David said.

"We gotta get out from under the branches," Xander said. He pointed at the sky. "We gotta go higher."

CHAPTER

thirty-three

WEDNESDAY, 12:51 P.M.

Hovering over the clearing with his brother and sister, David said, "I thought this was it. As high as we could go."

"We've only done this once before," Xander reminded him. "And we didn't try to go higher than the trees."

They kicked and paddled their way to the edge of the branches and leaves.

Whoop-whoop-whoop!

The rifle snapped through the fine branches, not a foot from David. A twig shot into his cheek. He reeled back, feeling the sting, as though slapped with a riding crop. "Ahh!"

Below, Phemus snatched the rifle out of the air. He moved around, searching for the best angle of attack.

Toria said, "David, you're bleeding."

He touched his face, looked at the blood on his fingers. He said, "That guy's three for three. He got us all."

"Come on," Xander said. He pointed his face toward the open sky beyond the foliage and paddled his injured hand in the air.

They began to rise. Their heads lifted over the branches. David and Xander shared a smile.

Like flipping from one photograph to another, Xander's expression instantly changed to panic. A second later David's did, too, as the firmness of the air that keep them aloft evaporated and they plunged down . . .

. . . below the forest canopy . . .

. . . and still they plummeted . . .

. . . down, down . . .

David had felt the same plummeting roller-coaster feel in his gut when he'd fallen all the way to the meadow and broken his arm. Only that time he'd been at the clearing's edge and was able to slow his fall by grabbing branches. No branches now, only a free fall to earth.

He closed his eyes and squeezed himself closer to his sister.

His mind betrayed him with a gruesome assessment of what was to come: Their legs would shatter. Their organs and bones, their spines and heads, would compact on themselves. They might splatter or simply crumple into skin-bags of what used to be David, Xander, and Toria. At least that way, they'd have separate coffins.

Against all hope, David kicked and paddled. The wind rushed past him. Then he felt it in his stomach: a lurching stop, like an elevator's but stronger.

He allowed one eye to open, then the other. They were ten feet from the ground and starting to rise again. Phemus ran toward them, swinging the rifle like a club.

"Kick," Xander said.

He hadn't needed to say it. David was already moving his legs and feet faster than he ever had.

Phemus hurled the rifle at them. It nicked David's sneaker, one of an old tattered pair he had to put on this morning because he'd lost one of his good Converses in the Civil War world. His little toe flared with pain, as though someone had stomped on it.

"We can't keep doing this," David said. "It's just a matter of time before one of us gets nailed good."

Whoop-whoop-whoop!

All of them heard it, none of them saw it coming. It sailed up from directly below them, this time spinning vertically, like a propeller—and just as deadly. It passed inches in front of them. If they had leaned their heads down to take a look, it would have clobbered them.

Clobbered? David thought. *No . . . it would have killed them.*

"We're fish in a barrel," Xander said.

"Look," Toria said.

David followed her gaze to the tangle of branches and leaves hung over the edge of the clearing. He said, "What?"

"The branches," she said. "See how thick they are over there. We can—"

"Yeah," Xander interrupted. "If we could get on top of them, we'd have some protection."

"Can we fly above them?" David wondered.

"Probably not," said Xander. "But we can *reach* them, and climb up onto them."

The rifle spun by—nowhere close, for a change.

"Let's do it," David said.

They made their way to the heaviest branch and hovered below it.

"Grab hold, Toria," Xander said. "Pull yourself up onto it. We'll give you a boost."

She released her death grip on David's neck and extended a shaking hand to the branch. The boys pushed her up.

None of them heard the rifle coming. It struck Xander's back. He let out a sharp groan, arched backward as though he'd taken a bullet in the chest, and fell.

CHAPTER

thirty-four

WEDNESDAY, 12:55 P.M.

Falling, Xander whirled his arms. He scissored his legs. His descent slowed and he started back up, not unlike a bungee jumper. Groaning, alternately reaching for his injury and paddling, Xander returned to the branch.

"You okay?" David said.

"I'll live . . . this time." He groaned, then said, "Toria, you good?"

She peered past the branch and nodded. Her arms clutched

the branch. "I want to hold my ankle, but I'm afraid to let go."

"Don't," David said.

Xander said, "Just remember to watch for that thing coming at you. Duck away from it, move your hands if you have to. But don't fall off."

"I'll get on the branch right behind her," David said. "I'll grab her if it looks like she's in trouble."

"Okay." Xander's face was twisted into a pained grimace.

"You sure you're all right?"

"I said I'll live, not that I'm all right." He grinned, but David could tell it was forced. "Get up there," Xander said. "I'll help."

David grabbed the branch behind Toria and kicked his feet. He floated up. Before he could swing his leg over, the air's firmness faltered and disappeared. Gravity pulled him down. Xander got his hand under David's rump and gave him a shove. He settled onto the branch just before the rifle smacked it directly under him, kicking up a spray of bark. The toy spun off, right over Xander's shoulder.

Xander reeled away from it. He drifted to the next branch, about ten feet away, and scrambled onto it. He held on with one hand and rubbed his back with the other.

Whoop-whoop-whoop!

The rifle flew up between the branches, tore away leaves, then went down again.

"Hey, Xander," David said. "Remember the weird movie title or whatever it was you thought of when the gladiator was spinning his swords at you?"

"Yeah, that's right," Xander said, remembering. "*Pinwheel of Death.*"

"Fits here, huh?"

The next throw came at the branch that Xander occupied, a foot away from his head. Xander released his grip, tucked his arms close to his body, then grabbed the branch again after the rifle's strike. In a deep voice, with precise diction, he said, "In a world where hiding in trees is the only way to survive, three children must learn to outsmart the . . . *Pinwheel of Death.*"

David smiled. Was it the clearing making them feel a little better, or did people in terrifying situations naturally think of things that calmed their fear? Either way, he liked the distraction. He said, "I don't think that's a movie I'd want to see anymore."

Toria saw the next one coming and tucked in perfectly. When the rifle clattered under David, it was he who almost lost his balance and tumbled off. Phemus must have decided he'd found a weak link; he continued targeting David, toss after toss.

Pulling his arms out of the way for what seemed like the hundredth time, David said, "Man, this is getting to me. Doesn't that guy have to go back to his own world sometime?"

Xander thought about it. "I thought Dad said the worlds had to balance out, eventually. Like the way the items in the antechambers pull toward the portal, and whatever we bring back with us gets sucked into its own world again. I kind of thought that worked with people too."

"Then why didn't Mom come back?" Toria said.

They didn't have an answer.

David closed his eyes, listening for the approaching Pinwheel of Death.

When there'd been no attacks for a few minutes, he opened his eyes. Xander looked asleep. Toria was gazing into the leaves farther along the branch, probably pretending she was looking out her bedroom window or . . . anywhere but balancing on a branch fifty feet in the air with some guy trying to knock her off it. He looked down.

"Oh . . . you gotta be kidding!" he said.

Xander raised his head, looked. "No!"

"What's he doing?" Toria said.

"He's flying."

CHAPTER thirty-five

WEDNESDAY, 1:10 P.M.

Phemus hovered two feet off the ground. He wobbled and dropped onto the grass. He prodded at the air with his toes. He hopped up, as though he'd felt something. He went right back down and tried again. It was a bit like watching a bodybuilder trying to tap dance, but there was nothing funny about it.

"Do you think he can do it?" Toria said.

"He'd better not," Xander said.

"He already did," David said. "If he floats up two feet, it's just a matter of time before he's coming up here."

As they watched, he did do it. Not for long, not very high, but he definitely sailed up for a few seconds.

"See?" David said.

"We're dead," Xander said. His eyes darted to Toria. "Uh . . . I mean . . . we'll figure something out."

"You can say *we're dead*," she said. "I'm not a baby."

"No, really," Xander said. "We'll figure—"

"Here he comes," David said.

The big man hovered five feet over the grass, wobbling, shifting one way, then the other. He grinned up at the kids, then looked down at his feet.

"Go away!" David yelled.

Phemus snapped his gaze up and crashed to the earth, sitting hard. He hoisted himself up, began feeling the air with his foot. He lifted into the air.

"Hey!" Xander said. "Go away!"

"Get out of here!" David screamed.

Toria simply screamed, a long piercing warble.

This time their attempts to distract him didn't hinder his flying at all. He hovered, slid sideways, came back . . . a little higher.

Xander cast a worried glance at David. He whispered, "I'll come over and get you. We'll both get Toria."

"Then what?" David said.

Xander shrugged. "Dodge away."

"Carrying Toria?"

"We have to try."

"Hey," David said. The bushes at the perimeter of the clearing rustled and parted. A man broke through and fell onto the grass. He eyed Phemus, who apparently hadn't heard his approach—then took in the kids.

"Keal!" David said.

"Help!" Toria yelled.

Keal leaped forward like a sprinter coming off the starting line. He ran directly for Phemus.

"The big guy's too high up," Toria said.

"We'll see," David said.

Keal sprang, sailing higher than anyone ever would have expected . . . anyone who didn't know the clearing. He grabbed Phemus's ankles and pulled the big man down. Phemus flashed a surprised expression and crashed to the earth. Keal was on him, landing punch after punch to the ribs, stomach, face. Phemus hammered a monstrous fist into Keal's back.

David knew too well what that fist felt like. His face still hurt. He said, "Phemus is too strong, even for Keal."

"Maybe not when he's away from the house," Xander said. "I get the feeling he *needs* the house . . . or the world he came from. That's why he keeps going back to it."

Hoping Xander was right this time, David yelled, "Get him, Keal!"

"Get him!" Toria echoed.

Keal dodged a blow. He flipped onto his back on the grass and kicked his heel into Phemus's face.

The big man's head snapped back. He rolled onto his stomach, rose onto his hands and knees, and started to stand.

Keal was already up. He kicked the man's head, shifted and kicked his ribs. He swung his right fist down into the back of Phemus's head.

David heard the *crack* and winced. He hoped the noise wasn't Keal's hand breaking.

If it was, Keal showed no sign. He swung his left fist into the side of Phemus's temple, then planted the right one between his shoulder blades. Keal meant business: He didn't pause, he didn't give his opponent a second to recover. He continued to pummel the man. Punch, punch, kick, punch, kick, kick.

Don't wanna ever get Keal mad at me, David thought.

Phemus swung his arm around, knocking Keal's leg out from under him. Keal went down, and Phemus grabbed his foot. He pulled Keal to him and brought a fist down onto his stomach. Keal wheezed out a gust of air, buckled in half. Phemus swung a fist into Keal's head. Keal did what every fighter does when the blows are landing and he can't get away. He dove into his opponent, hugging him, giving him no room to swing.

They rolled in the grass—and lifted off it. David squinted,

and yes, the two men were tumbling in the air, three or four feet off the ground. Rising higher.

Phemus pushed Keal away. Keal did a backward somersault and stood. He almost fell over, caught himself, and looked down at the grass a half dozen feet below him. He wobbled. He turned a stunned face at the kids.

"Keep going, Keal!" Xander yelled.

"Move like you're underwater!" David told him.

Phemus slid through the air. He reached his opponent and clamped his arms around Keal's torso. The silent scream Keal displayed indicated that Phemus was squeezing him. David could only imagine how much pressure those tree-trunk arms could exert.

Keal began punching Phemus's ear. His knees came up into Phemus's gut. They broke away from each other only to embrace again: Keal encircled his muscular left arm around Phemus's neck. He pounded his right fist into the big man's face, again and again.

Phemus landed one blow after another into Keal's stomach and sides. Without pausing in his face-pounding, Keal kicked at Phemus's crotch.

All the while, the men tumbled and rose through the air. They were in the center of the clearing, measured aerially as well as across its breadth and width. It almost seemed staged to David, but the sounds of their blows and grunts, as well as the blood and sweat flying off them, said otherwise.

Phemus reached behind his back, fumbled with something at the small of his back, where the pelt started, and pulled out a black shardlike object.

"Keal!" David yelled. "He has a knife!"

Phemus raise the blade and plunged it down.

Keal grabbed the big man's wrist. He never released his arm from Phemus's neck. Phemus never ceased in slamming his fist into Keal's ribs. Phemus's arm looked like a machine *pumping pumping pumping.*

David threw himself off the branch. He plunged down five feet, ten feet. He felt the resistance in the air and started kicking, swimming with his arms.

"David!" Toria yelled.

He ignored her and continued moving toward the fighting men. He circled them, keeping himself directly behind Phemus. When he saw his chance, he sailed in and grabbed the hand that held the knife. He could see now that it was a chiseled piece of black stone.

Keal saw David, saw him holding the knife hand. He let go of Phemus's wrist, pulled back, and brought his fist into the big man's nose.

David strained against Phemus's hand that was trying to plunge the knife into Keal. He squeezed his eyes closed and concentrated on not letting that happen. He rose up over the men's heads. He kicked, using the motion to help him keep the knife high in the air, high above Keal.

He heard a *crack!* and looked. Xander was hovering behind Phemus, holding the barrel of the toy rifle. He had apparently retrieved it from the ground and batted the stock into the back of the big man's head. He cocked it back for another strike.

Phemus twisted out of Keal's headlock. He lifted his foot, planted it on Keal's sternum, and pushed off. He sailed away, taking David with him and banging into Xander. Xander spun away, twirling like a top. Phemus dropped straight down, wrenching his hand out of David's grasp. The stone knife slid through David's fingers. David gasped and pulled his hands back.

As he fell, Phemus lunged at Keal, stretching his knife toward him. Keal kicked away, but the blade caught his leg, ripping through his pant leg. Phemus continued falling—all the way to the grass, twenty-five feet below. He landed with a grunt and rolled. He hopped up, glaring at the boys and man above him. Then he ran to the edge of the clearing and disappeared into the bushes.

CHAPTER thirty-six

WEDNESDAY, 1:22 P.M.

Breathing hard, Keal kept his eyes on the spot where Phemus had disappeared. He drifted and bobbed in the air like a ping-pong ball on the surface of a lake.

David drifted to him and reached out to touch his shoulder.

Keal jerked around, raising a fist. Registering David, he smiled.

"Thank you," David said. He noticed red fingerprints

where he'd touched Keal and looked at his palm. Blood covered his hand, glistening.

"I think his blade was obsidian," Keal said. "Sharper than a razor, so it probably doesn't hurt much, does it?"

Watching the slice across his palm open and shut like a mouth as he flexed his hand, David shook his head.

"It'll take forever to heal, though," Keal said. He rubbed the side of his face, then stuck a finger in his mouth to wiggle a tooth. He spat, watching the bloody goop fall to the grass far below. He said, "This is weirdest thing I've ever experienced."

Xander bumped into David. He said, "You ain't seen nothing yet."

Keal studied the boys' faces, perhaps looking for signs of humor. He tightened his lips and nodded. "I'll be right back." He waved his arms and drifted down.

"How's your back?" David asked his brother.

"Hurts. This too." Xander showed him the back of his hand. The purple had taken on hues of blue, black, and red.

David scowled at it. He said, "I think we've been banged up worse in this world than in any of the others."

They watched Keal reach the grass and trudge into the bushes at the clearing.

"It's *because* of those other worlds that we've been attacked in this one," Xander said. "Taksidian wants the house because of them, and he's doing everything he can to get it."

Toria's tiny voice reached them: "Hey, guys?"

They smiled at each other. Xander said, "Be kind of funny to leave her there a while."

David backhanded Xander's shoulder. "Not."

They sailed up to her. David could tell she'd been crying. It must have been scary, watching the fight. David and Xander each rested a hand on the branch, like swimmers at the edge of the pool. Their legs stirred gently, as they would have in water.

"Xander," David said. "Why do you think Taksidian wants it, the house?"

"A house like that," Xander said. "It's pretty special."

"We just want to get Mom and get out," David said. "We don't want it. He must plan on using it for something. What?"

Xander's brow crunched in thought, squeezing out a drop of blood from the cut on his forehead. "He told us he'd been in the house many times. He's probably been doing something here for a long time. He doesn't like that we're here now, keeping him from continuing whatever it is."

"I want down," Toria said.

"Come on," Xander said.

The brothers turned their backs to the branch so she could wrap her arms around their shoulders and swing down between them. They reached across with their free arms, held each other's hand, and pulled themselves together.

Toria giggled. "Group hug," she said.

As they descended, Keal reappeared through the bushes, carrying Jesse. He was limping.

"Where were *you*?" David called. His voice was Mickey Mouse-ish.

Jesse laughed. It was squeaky, but only slightly so, there on the edge of the clearing. "In the woods. We saw the open front door and the collapsed walls on the second floor, knew you were in trouble. I was worried you'd gone the other way, into one of the worlds. Then we heard you yelling."

The children touched down in front of the men. As soon as the boys released Toria, she said, "Owww!" and crumpled to her knees.

"Toria, I forgot about your ankle," David said. He knelt beside her and helped her to sit.

"What is it, child?" Jesse said.

Keal set the old man on the grass beside her. The big man groaned and touched his ribs, his face, his stomach. "Feel like I had it out with the Terminator."

Xander smiled. If you wanted to get on his good side fast, reference a movie.

Toria pulled up her pant leg and slipped off her sneaker and sock. Her ankle looked like Xander's hand. It was black and blue and swollen to the size of a softball.

Keal dropped to his knees in front of her. "Can you move it?"

She turned her foot in a tight circle, making an *Eeeeee* sound the whole time.

The man prodded it, watching for her reactions. "It's not broken," he said. "Maybe sprained. Sure is a nasty bruise."

"Keal's a nurse," Jesse said. "A mighty good one too. Better than most doctors I've known."

"A *nurse*?" Xander said. "You?"

Keal looked up. He leaned back to rest on his ankles. "Now why would that surprise you?"

"It's just . . ." Xander said. "You know."

Keal stared at him, said nothing.

Xander said, "I mean, you're big enough to be a linebacker, you got the muscles of a bodybuilder, and you fight like . . . like some kind of special forces commando."

Keal laughed. He settled into a sitting position on the grass and crossed his leg in front of him. He poked his fingers into the tear Phemus's knife had made and ripped the material through the cuff. He flipped the two sides away, revealing a long gash in his shin from knee to ankle.

His dark brown skin made it difficult for David to tell how much it had bled.

Keal poked at the wound and said, "Well, I was an athlete back in the day. I also served my country, and I enjoy keeping physically fit. As for my profession, by the time I ruled out those other occupations, I was a little too old to pursue a medical degree. But I do like helping people."

He glanced at Xander, who nodded.

David said, "You saved our lives."

Keal smiled. "Looked like you were doing a pretty good job of that yourselves."

"Still," Xander said, "we owe you."

"It was a team effort, gentlemen," Keal said. "I appreciate your help too. Let's call it even."

Xander stepped past Keal to hold his good hand out to Jesse. He curled his fingers around the old man's hand and said, "I'm sorry I doubted you. I guess you are on our side."

Jesse nodded. "Quite understandable, Xander. In fact, I consider your caution both admirable and necessary."

Xander smiled and released Jesse's hand, but the old man refused to let go.

Jesse said, "Does this mean, Xander, that you're ready to confide in me? I can help, but I need to know . . . where are your parents? What has been going on around here?"

Xander's smile faded, but he nodded. Jesse gave him back his hand, and Xander straightened. He rubbed his back, grimacing at the pain still there. He said, "We need to get back to the house. I don't want to be away from it too long, and there may be things we need to show you, if you want to know everything."

"The more I know, the more I can help," Jesse said.

"Okay." Xander looked toward the house. "But . . . do you think they're waiting for us, those guys we fought?"

"More than one?" Keal said.

"Three," Xander said. "Two stayed in the house."

"They're gone," Jesse said. "Keal and I went all through it, looking for you. And I'm sure that one you chased out of here is back where he belongs by now. Visitors don't stay long. They can't. Unless . . ."

"Unless?" Xander said.

Jesse waved a hand at him. "That's for another time. First things first."

"But what if they come back?" Toria said.

"They will," David said. "They *attacked* us. They knocked down the walls. They'll be back."

Jesse shook his head. "They can't. Not for a while. They'll have to sort of *recharge*. It's draining, going over. For them and for us. Haven't you noticed that?"

Xander said, "Remember, Dae, how tired I was after the gladiator thing, and you after the jungle world?"

David nodded. "The showers helped." To Jesse, he said, "Does using the portals make you . . . I don't know . . . more emotional?"

"Crying a lot?" Jesse said with a knowing smile.

"Sort of," David said, shrugging shyly.

"I know how you feel," Jesse said, "but it's not the portals. Not really. It's your *humanity*, David. Going over, you see things most people never do. Terrible atrocities, the worst human behavior. Murder, war, innocence lost. You have a big heart for people. Of course, you're part of the King bloodline—you have to."

"What does that mean?"

"You'll find out . . . in time." Jesse winked. "I'm not trying to be mysterious. It's just that there are other things I need to explain first. It's like constructing the first floor of a house before adding the second."

"Are you saying I'm *sensitive*?" David said, not liking it much. "That's why I've been crying?"

"No," Jesse said. "I'm saying it breaks your heart when people die before their time, because they'll never get to be everything they could have been."

"That sounds like David," Toria said. "He's sad when people get hurt on TV."

"Am not," David said.

"Uh-huh."

"It's okay that you do," Jesse said. "You have a keen sense of the preciousness of life and the finality of death—here on earth, anyway. To you, death does not simply end life. It steals away the sunsets you'll never see, the children you'll never hold, the wife you'll never love. It's frightening to almost lose your future, and it's heartbreaking to witness death snuff out other people's tomorrows." He gripped David's shoulder. "You get it? What's making you cry comes from the same place inside that prompted you to save Marguerite's life. You weep for life lost, and you *act* to prevent it."

David rocked up on his knees and wrapped his arms around Jesse's neck. No one had ever so accurately described his desire for himself and others to experience the fullest possible life; or the ache in his chest at the news of death—by accident, murder, war. Even *he* hadn't put it into words. Now that Jesse had, he recognized it as a grand quality. He hoped he could live up to it.

CHAPTER

thirty-seven

WEDNESDAY, 1:36 P.M.

Grunting with effort, Xander struggled to stand. When he finally did, he said, "We gotta head back."

David released his embrace on Jesse's neck and rolled back onto the grass.

Jesse peered around the clearing, rising to take in the trees and canopy. He turned to Xander and said, "I'll give you the rest of my time on earth. Just give me a few minutes now. Can you do that?"

Xander sighed. He stepped past Jesse and Keal and sat beside his sister.

Jesse touched David's arm. "Son, would you mind giving me a hand?"

"I don't think I can pick you up," David said.

"The clearing will help," Jesse said.

David rose and stepped behind him. He slipped his hands under Jesse's arms and lifted. The old man was light, impossibly light.

Jesse's legs dangled under him. His feet were canted at odd angles on the ground.

Walking behind him, David guided Jesse toward the center of the meadow.

"Oh," Jesse said, "it's been so long."

As they progressed, the weight bearing down on David's arms—accompanied by a slight throbbing in the broken one—became less noticeable. Before long, he was pretty sure he wasn't assisting Jesse at all. He realized that his hands, positioned in Jesse's armpits, had risen to the level of his eyes, as though the man had grown taller. He saw that Jesse's feet no longer touched the ground, but hovered a few inches above it.

"Thank you, son," Jesse said, his voice comically high. "I can manage from here."

David lowered his hands slowly, and when Jesse didn't come down with them, he backed away.

Jesse waved his hands and turned. The grin on his face lightened David's heart.

David looked back at the others, his own smile bigger than it should have been, considering . . . *everything*. He was glad to see Keal, Toria, even Xander, looking equally pleased.

Jesse drifted up and laughed, a squeaky cartoon hiccup sound. As Dad had done, he zipped forty feet over and twenty feet in the air. Returning, he performed a somersault—perfect but for his legs, which trailed his body loosely like a those of a ventriloquist's puppet. He buzzed around, soaring high, spinning, brushing his fingers along the canopy leaves. After five minutes he came down on the far side of the clearing. Watching his feet skimming the grass, he drifted toward them, laughing continually.

Drawing near, he said, "I haven't walked in a decade. This is as close as I'll ever come again."

CHAPTER

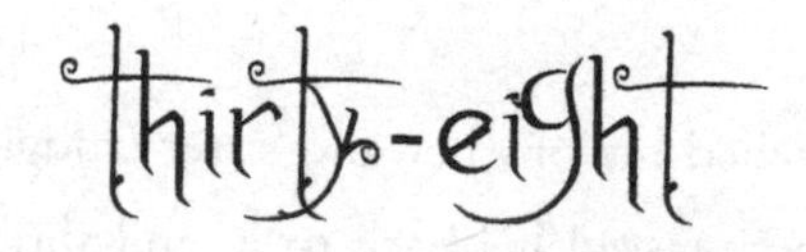

WEDNESDAY, 1:46 P.M.

Xander carried Toria through the woods, toward the house. Behind them, Keal carried Jesse. David walked beside them.

"What you told me before," David said, "about my being part of the King bloodline? You know, so I *have* to be the way I am, that I care for people, love life? Does that have to do with being a gatekeeper?"

Jesse bounced along in Keal's arms, thinking. He said, "I

shouldn't have told you that so soon. I was just excited, seeing you and all."

"But . . . does it mean we're supposed to stay here? Like you did?"

"That's a discussion we should have with your mom and dad," Keal said.

David stopped.

Keal took another two steps and turned to him.

"My mom's gone," David said.

"Gone?" Jesse squinted at him. "What do you mean, son?"

David watched his brother and sister trudging away. He went to a tree, pressed his back to it, and slid down. "The other night, that guy we fought—Xander and I call him Phemus—he came out of a portal and took her." He looked into Jesse's eyes. The story came rushing out.

"He kidnapped my mother. Took her back into one of the worlds with him. We didn't know which. We've been looking, but all this other stuff has been getting in the way. This guy's trying to get us out of the house . . . he sent those—those *things* after us . . . got Dad arrested . . . people—a kid—found out about the house, the portals . . . and . . . and . . ."

His lungs were pumping fast and hard. Tears streamed from his eyes.

Keal stepped back and settled Jesse onto the ground in front of David. Jesse's kind face had morphed into one of supreme sadness. Not shock, just an expression like that David had seen on TV news reporters when they covered the funerals of children. A phrase he'd heard came to mind: *profound grief.*

Jesse reached out and touched David's shoe. "I am so sorry, David."

David sniffed. He wiped the back of his hands across his eyes. "There I go again," he said with an embarrassed smile.

"Kid," Keal said, "if I were you, I'd be bawling like a baby."

From much closer to the house, Xander called: "David? What's up?"

"Go on!" David yelled. "We'll be there in a minute!"

They listened for a response. When it didn't come, Jesse said, "When you're ready, I'd like to hear everything. Start at the beginning."

David closed his eyes, took a deep breath, and started. He told about their drive to Pinedale, house hunting, setting foot in the creepy old Victorian for the first time. He told about discovering that the linen closet was a portal to the locker at school. His voice rose a bit when he recounted their discovery of the antechambers, the items within them, and Xander's trip to the Colosseum. He told about his own trip to the jungle world, where tigers and tribesmen tried to kill him.

At this point, David closed his eyes again. He bit his lip, tightened his muscles and his resolve, and went on: Waking up to Toria screaming that a man had been in her room. Mom getting taken, and how they'd all been beat up trying to stop Phemus.

"That's when we found out Dad had lied about the house. He had known about the portals and how dangerous it was." David covered his eyes with his hand. "He just wanted to find *his* mother."

Then they had vowed to stay in the house and rescue Mom, despite Dad's dad giving up on finding *Dad's* mother and leaving. He talked about setting up the Mission Control Center ("we call it the MCC"). Dad showing them what they could do in the clearing. Then Taksidian: his seeing David fly and David breaking his arm because of it. David going through the locker portal and finding Taksidian in their house talking to Phemus. Taksidian chasing him back through to the locker and how Xander and he had locked him inside. The doctor accusing Dad of hurting his kids. The town trying to evict them. Xander and he going to the Civil War world.

And then last night's events ("I can't believe it was only last night"): Dad getting arrested, Clayton coming through the locker-to-closet portal, Xander saying he'd found Mom.

"But he *hadn't,*" David said. "She'd left a message for us, but when I went back to get her, I got chased away . . . *shot* at . . . *again.*"

Jesse aimed watery, sympathetic eyes at David. And David thought that if a twig snapped, or a door burst open, Keal would jump right out of his skin. They sat like that, silent and listening to their own breathing and wind touching the treetops.

Finally Jesse took a deep breath. "You astound me," he said. "Your bravery, your family's determination."

David could offer up only a weak smile. He said, almost desperately, "Can you help?"

Don't say maybe. Don't say maybe. Don't say maybe.

"Yes, I can," Jesse said.

It was what he had needed to hear since the moment the door had slammed shut on the bat and their mother's screams. This time, David's smile was genuine and big.

Jesse patted David's foot. "Let's get on with it, then, shall we?" He looked over his shoulder. "Keal?"

The man snapped out of some daydream, surely involving kidnapped mothers and evil villains. "Yeah, yeah," he said, standing. "On with it."

Worried eyes landed on David, and David understood that Keal was as clueless about what to do—what Jesse *could* do—as he was.

Keal scooped up Jesse. He stood there, waiting for David, who wasn't so sure his own legs would work if he tried to stand. He felt as though he had gone through all the events of the past week in the fifteen minutes it had taken to describe them. But he pushed himself up, and his legs did work. He fell in beside Keal and Jesse, and they walked to the house.

CHAPTER

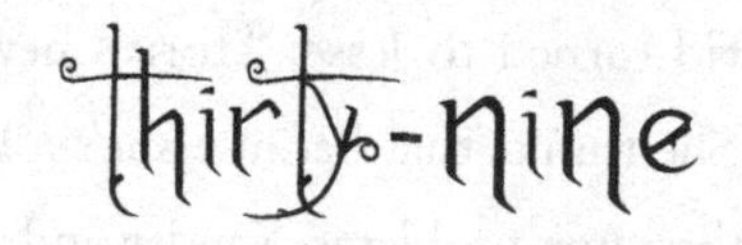

WEDNESDAY, 2:11 P.M.

They found Xander and Toria sitting on the front porch steps.

"I told them everything," David said.

"I know," Xander said. He looked at Keal and Jesse, trying to read their expressions.

"Jesse said he can help."

"*Can* you?" Xander asked the old man.

"Absolutely."

Xander smiled at that. He rose and headed for the front door, Toria right behind him. David stopped at the bottom.

"What are you going to do?" David asked, though he had a pretty good hunch.

"Get Mom," Xander said.

"You mean you're sending *Toria* to get her," David said. "You can't do that."

"Dae, we agreed. We said today, this morning, remember? It's always been about Toria going over."

"But—" David turned to Jesse. "Toria's never been into another world. She thinks that because she's a little girl, she won't run into the same problems Xander and I did."

Jesse looked up at Xander. "That may not be true, Xander. You've noticed a lot of aggression toward you in those other worlds, right?"

"Have we!" David said. "Everywhere we go someone's trying to kill us. I'm *twelve*. Do I look like a soldier? Do I look like a spy? But General Grant shot at me! And he wasn't the only one—"

Jesse was patting the air in front of him, telling David to calm down.

"You were wearing the wrong colors when we first went over," Xander protested. "And in World War II, you walked into the middle of a firefight."

Jesse waved his hand at Xander. "Boys! Yes, the circumstances you walk into have a lot to do with whether you're in danger. But it's more than that. You may *look* like you belong when you go over, but you don't. The people over there sense that. Like there's something not right about you."

David thought about the hostile looks the soldiers in the Civil War camp had given him—even though they could see he was a child. And the tribesmen who had immediately thrown spears and shot arrows at him; he hadn't threatened them in any way.

He said, "See? Xander, they'll sense that about Toria. You can't let her go. Jesse, tell him!"

Jesse frowned. "David—"

David saw it in his face: he was about to agree with Xander! "Jesse, you just said—"

"David, if she gets in and right back out . . . it *would* be hard for those men over there to mistake her for a soldier."

David's shoulders slumped.

Behind him, Xander said, "Come on, Toria."

"Wait, wait!" David said. "Toria, you heard what Jesse said. Do you still want to go?"

She made a face that said *Not really*. But she nodded.

"Your ankle! How can you go with your ankle like that?"

"I can walk," she said.

"But you can't run. I haven't been in a world where I haven't had to run."

She simply stared at him, a tight little frown bending her lips.

David didn't care about being outvoted. He just didn't want his sister to go. Not there. Not to *any* of the worlds. But what more could he say?

Jesse said, "I'm sorry, David. Maybe the portal won't come around before we get back, but if—"

"Where are you going?"

"To get your daddy out of jail. I have experience with small-town authorities, thinking they can do anything they wish."

"Xander!" David turned to his brother, then back to Jesse. "Tell them to wait. Dad can go get Mom. They don't know him in that world."

"Thing is," Jesse said, "I don't think they should wait. You mother being lost over there, taken against her will, without any way of finding the portal home—getting her out of there quickly is worth the risk. And given Toria's age and how short of a time she should be there . . ." He looked up to her. "Just in and out, right, young lady?"

"Yes, sir," Toria said.

"David," Jesse continued, "if you weigh the possibility of your mother disappearing forever against the possibility of Toria having some trouble, I think you'll agree. What I'm saying is: get her while you can, however you can."

CHAPTER

WEDNESDAY, 3:28 P.M.

David stood rigid at the head of the third-floor hallway, his arms crossed over his chest. Jesse's points were hard to argue with, but Toria wasn't *his* sister.

Xander and Toria marched up and down the crooked hall, checking each antechamber for the Civil War items.

Come on, Dad. Where are you?

They'd been up on the third floor over an hour now. How long did it take to get Dad out of jail?

Xander looked his way, and David changed his worried face to an angry scowl.

"This would be faster if you helped," Xander said.

"I don't want it to be faster," David said. "I don't want it at all."

Xander stopped, the handle of an open door in his hand. He said, "Well, don't get any ideas."

"Like what?"

"Like trying to stop her from going over when we find the right portal."

"At least wait until Dad gets home."

"Nice try," Xander said. "You know Dad wouldn't let her go."

"Which should tell you something."

"It does." Xander opened a door, peered inside, closed it. "That Dad is so cautious, we might never find Mom."

David bit his tongue. Xander wasn't going to listen to anything he had to say.

His brother frowned. "Come on, Dae," he said. "When I was mad at Dad for lying to us about the house, you said we had to get along. Work together. You were right. I'm not mad at you for disagreeing with me now, but you're being pigheaded."

"About Toria's life?" David said. "Yeah, I am."

"You heard Jesse. What might happen to Toria is less awful than what might happen to Mom if we don't find her."

"What's worse than death?"

"She's not going to die."

Xander checked the antechamber closest to David, then headed back the other way. He said, "What if it takes days for Jesse to get Dad out, Dae? What if something happens to Mom while we're waiting? Could you live with that?"

Toria was hobbling from door to door, staying off her banged-up ankle as much as she could.

"Toria," David said. "Don't do this."

She walked toward him, making a sad face. "I don't like you and Xander fighting."

"Then don't go. Tell him you changed your mind."

"But Xander's right," she said. "We need to get Mom, Dae. The people over there won't recognize me." She touched his arm. "I'll be careful, and I'll come right back if it gets scary. I promise."

David went to the landing. It looked as though a bomb had gone off at the base of the stairs. The two walls had collapsed into the second-floor hallway. Wires and studs jutted out from where the walls used to stand, and plaster dust covered it all.

"Got it!" Xander said.

The words hit David's gut like a one-two punch.

Toria shut the door she had just opened, looked at Xander standing in the doorway of an antechamber halfway up the hall. She turned back to David, fear on her face.

Both boys called to her at the same moment.

She went toward Xander.

Five minutes later, she wore both jackets, the Union blue over the Confederate gray.

Xander told her, "If you wind up on the Confederate side, switch them. When you get to the Union side, switch back. But you should come out in the woods right near the camp, so no sweat. In camp, take off the jackets and fold them up. Carry them like you're taking them to get cleaned or something. Your kepi too."

He spun around, grabbed the blue hat from a hook, and pulled it down over her head. It covered her eyes, and she pushed it up.

"I think they're back," David said, though he had heard nothing. He ran to the antechamber's hallway door. "Really," he said. "Wait up and see." He called out: "Dad!"

Behind him, the portal door opened.

Toria and Xander stood in front of the portal. Bright sunlight poured through, along with the odor of smoke and gunpowder. Out-of-focus trees and bushes drifted slowly past.

"It looks like the woods by the camp," Xander told her. "Just like I said. Don't lose the clothes. They'll show you where the portal home is. They'll pull you toward it. It's that simple. You ready?"

"Toria," David said.

But she had stepped through.

He ran to the doorway.

She was lying in tall, yellow grass—she must have tumbled when she stepped through. Nothing unusual about that.

He yelled, "Come right back if you don't find Mom right away!"

Toria squinted at him, and stood. "What?" Her voice wavered, as though caught by the wind.

"David!" Xander said.

The door struck him in the back. It always closed on its own after someone went through. It knocked him into the door frame and pushed him as forcefully as the grill of a semi truck.

Xander grabbed his arm and yanked. David spun back into the room, and the door slammed shut.

CHAPTER

forty-one

WEDNESDAY, 4:09 P.M.

David sat on the bench, his eyes fixed on the portal door. His fingernails were absently scraping his plaster cast. He had flaked a groove into it and found some cloth gauze encased within. He fingers now flicked at this, tearing an ever-widening hole.

Xander paced. He walked to the portal door, spun, and walked through the opposite doorway into the hall. He marched back through and did it again.

Neither brother had spoken since Toria had left.

Finally David said, "It's been twenty minutes."

"Almost," Xander said, continuing his back-and-forth strolling.

"Longer," David said. "Xander, something must have happened to her."

"Give her a chance, Dae. She'll be back any minute, wait and see. And with Mom." Now he did stop. His face was alive with excitement. He really believed Toria would find Mom and bring her home.

Xander's belief infected David. He allowed himself to *feel* it, to feel that Mom really was on her way. He could almost smell her, that hint of flowers that seemed natural to her. He imagined throwing his arms around her, squeezing her. He would never let her go.

As worried as he was, he smiled back at Xander.

Somewhere in the house, a door slammed.

"Dad!" David said. He jumped off the bench. Both boys ran into the hall and stopped on the landing. "Dad!" David yelled again. "Jesse!"

No reply.

They turned big eyes on each other. "You think," David said, "maybe it's those big guys again, the ones from the other world?"

Xander shook his head. "They'd come from one of the rooms up here. Besides, Jesse said Phemus couldn't come back so soon."

They returned to the antechamber, and David took up his spot on the bench. He swallowed hard and glanced nervously at the open door. Xander walked to the portal door, tried the handle—locked, of course.

Another bang. David jumped.

Xander gave David a puzzled look and went into the hall. "Dad?" he called. He walked away from the antechamber.

David went to the doorway and peered out.

Xander was standing halfway to the landing, listening. "Probably just the house trying to spook us," he said.

"It's working," David said.

"Could be just the wind," Xander said. " I'll go check." But he didn't move, just stood there, as if expecting David to say, "Nah, never mind."

Instead, David said, "Okay."

Xander smiled. He walked to the landing, then tromped down the stairs.

David watched for a few seconds, then he scanned the hallway. All the other doors were closed, as they were supposed to be. He glanced over his shoulder at the portal door Toria had used.

Twenty, twenty-five minutes she'd been gone. That was too long.

He had an idea. Xander would never let him do it, but hey, he was downstairs. Dad would call it *impulsive*—doing something simply because the chance presented itself. It was unplanned, stupid.

Not stupid this time, David thought. *Not when it's been almost a half hour.*

He slipped into the antechamber, plucked a canteen and the gray kepi off their hooks, and picked up a sword from the bench. He opened the portal door—unlocked now that he held the items—and stepped through.

• • • • • • • •

David ran through the woods toward the meadow of dry grass and the Union army camp on the other side. He could not see much activity among the tents: one or two people walking along the center aisle. Most of the soldiers must be at the front lines. He wished he'd had time to research the Civil War, especially the Union side and its encampments and battle policies, before plunging into it again. But they'd hardly had time to grab a few hours' sleep, let alone do homework.

At the edge of the woods, he dropped the sword into the grass. As he tucked the kepi into his waistband, he looked around for landmarks that would help him find the sword again.

That tree, he thought. *Split, as though by lightning.*

He hoped the pull of the kepi and canteen, and the items Toria had brought, would be enough to guide them to the portal home.

He bolted for the tents. Before he reached them, he heard a scream coming from the front of the camp. *Toria.*

He angled that direction through the field. He reached the back of the first tent and stopped.

Toria was crying. Men were laughing.

David's guts felt twisted. He looked around the edge of the tent. Toria was walking slowly away from two soldiers. She was limping, trying to avoid putting weight on her injured ankle. She wore the blue kepi and jacket, and she was heading south, toward the hill over which David knew the battle raged. And she was carrying a rifle!

The gun was longer than she was tall. She had not brought it over with her. The Harper's Ferry rifle David had used on his first venture to this world was still in the antechamber when he left. She kept glancing back over her shoulder.

The two soldiers followed twenty paces behind, laughing and pointing their rifles at her. Both weapons were fitted with long bayonets.

One soldier yelled at her, "Skedaddle, sweetie! Get out there and fight! Else we'll have to shoot you ourselves." He laughed, stopped, and jabbed the bayonet at her, though she was way out of striking distance.

"Everyone fights!" the soldier said. "Even country gals like you. No excuses!" He turned to his compatriot, a big grin on his face.

The other man yelled, "We don't wanna see you coming back

'less it's on a stretcher. You go all the way! Kill you some graybacks, then we'll think about letting you into camp."

The first soldier spotted David running toward him. "Hey, what's this?" he said, and swung the rifle around.

David didn't slow down. He swung his arm cast at the bayonet, knocking it aside. He jumped and shoved his palms into the soldier's chest. The man backpedaled and fell.

"David!" Toria ran to him. She tossed the rifle away and threw her arms around his neck.

"Woo-woo!" the standing soldier said. "Young love!"

"She's my *sister,*" David said. "What do you think you're doing? She's a little girl."

The downed man regained his feet. He picked up his rifle but held it vertically, casually. David thought his fury had startled the meanness out of the man, at least for the moment.

The soldier said, "Well, then, we have *two* greenhorns to send to the front, don't we?"

"We're friends with General Grant," David said. "Where is he? General Grant! General Grant!"

"Whoa, young master," the second solder said. "The general is in battle. Young lady, why didn't you say you knew the general?"

"Both of you!" David said. "I'm reporting both of you!" He grabbed Toria's hand and led her past the men into the camp.

He looked back. The soldiers were standing together, whispering. One of them scratched his head.

"You didn't find her?" David said.

"No," Toria said. "I saw Bob. He was drawn on the tent, like Xander said. And the message Mom left. I looked into a tent, and those two saw me. They started pushing me around, and one of them said I should be fighting."

"They're idiots," David said. Then he yelled, "Mom! Mom!"

"I thought we were supposed to be secret?"

"Who cares now? Let's find her and get out of here. I've had enough of this place. Mom!"

Toria took up the call: "Mom!"

The soldiers they'd left were heading for them. Something had them suspicious—maybe it was nothing more than what Jesse had said, that he and Toria weren't supposed to be there, and they sensed it.

David yelled again. "Mrs. King! Gertrude King!"

The soldiers were closing in.

"Ignore them," David told Toria. They continued toward the rear of the camp. With her limp, Toria's gait was more of a skip than a walk.

"Mom!" Toria yelled.

"Mrs. King!"

"You two!" the soldier behind them said. "You stop right there."

David turned to face them.

The one he'd knocked down said, "Doesn't sound like you're looking for General Grant. I don't think you're friends with the man. In fact, I don't think you even know him." He stepped closer, the bayonet five feet from David's chest. "Sammy, I think we got us some spies. Oooo, those gray-backs are getting tricky, sending kids."

The other soldier said, "You know what we do with spies?"

"Shoot on sight," the first man said.

"David?" Toria whispered.

An older woman, wearing a blood-covered smock, ran out from a nearby tent. She stopped between David and the bayonet. She faced the soldiers, put her fists on her hips, and said, "What do you think you're doing?"

"Well, ma'am . . ."

"These are *children!*" She pointed toward the front of the camp. "Go, both of you, before I have you thrown into the stockades!"

The two soldiers looked at each other, then back at the woman. Their shoulders slumped. They turned and walked away like five-year-olds heading for time-out.

As she watched them depart, she pulled off the soiled smock, crumpled it, and dropped it on the ground. Then she spun around.

David said, "Thank y—"

She darted toward them, grabbing the material over their

chests with her fists. She brought her nose to within an inch of Toria's, then did the same to David. Her eyes were huge, bright and blue.

Through gritted teeth, she said, "Did you say *King*?"

CHAPTER

forty-two

WEDNESDAY, 4:25 P.M.

Whatever had made the noises that drew him away, Xander hadn't found it. But when he returned to the Civil War antechamber, David was gone. One look at the hooks, with their missing items, told him that David had gone over.

I'll never figure that kid out, he thought.

He swirled his hands lightly against the grain of the portal door. He willed it to open, to admit back to their rightful time and place his brother and sister.

He could not believe what David had done. That . . . that . . . *punk*! And *he* had called Xander stupid! Xander had merely wanted to find Mom, and sending Toria seemed like the best way to do it. How much more stupid was it to go into a world where the people had chased you out with guns—twice?

When David returned, he was going to punch him, punch him hard.

No, he wasn't going to do that.

It was a brave thing to do, going over for Toria like that. What was with that kid? He would stand behind Xander if a shadow crept up the wall. But then he'd plunge into World War II and the Civil War, where you had to be afraid of a lot more than shadows. When the stakes were high, the outcome crucial, he manned up—because that's when bravery mattered.

Xander's mind kept casting images of all the things that could happen to his brother over there—unpretty things that would make a movie R-rated for "graphic violence."

Stop! He'll be fine.

He sat on the bench, put his hands on his knees, then stood again. He walked to the portal door, then into the hall.

Where was Dad?

Xander and David had shared a room their entire lives. They'd shared vacations and friends and baths. But over the past few years they hadn't spent much time hanging out.

David had his soccer and video games. Xander's interests were becoming more adult—or at least more older-teen: a girlfriend, making movies, driving.

But as they had faced a mutual enemy—the move itself, and then the house—Xander realized that David had been growing and maturing too. He had sharp ideas and a witty sense of humor, and generally gave as good as he got. His brother was someone he truly *liked,* not just loved.

So maybe, when he next saw David, he would give the kid a bone-crushing bear hug. *Then* he would punch him. Hard.

Toria, he would hug and spare the punch. He had to keep believing what he had told David: The people over there would see nothing more than a cute little girl. No threat. No one to throw in jail or shoot at. Her going over was much safer than David's.

He lowered his head into his hands.

The portal door burst open. Sunlight blinded Xander. Shadows cut through the radiance and slapped down on the antechamber floor, followed by tumbling, grunting, air rushing out of lungs. Sand and leaves blew in on smoky currents. The door slammed shut.

Toria sprang up at him and threw her arms around his neck. "Oh, Xander," she said. "It was awful! If David hadn't come, I would have . . . I . . ." She began to weep.

Xander squeezed her. Peering over her shoulder, he saw David lifting himself off the floor.

Then Xander's heart leaped. There was another person on the floor behind David. A woman. She had her hand pressed to her forehead; her hair hung over her face.

He shifted Toria to the bench beside him. When he turned back, the woman flipped her hair away from her face and looked at him.

His hope popped like a balloon. This was worse than not getting anything for Christmas, worse than not passing your driver's test, worse than being rejected by a girl you'd liked all year and finally summoned the courage to ask out.

It wasn't Mom.

The woman was old, a lot older than Mom. She was breathing heavily through her mouth, which had formed into a curious smile. But she had kind, vibrant eyes that somehow looked familiar.

Xander looked from the woman to David and back to the woman. Finally he said, "Who are you?"

"Are you Xander?" she said, pushing a strand of hair off her face.

Hesitantly, he nodded.

"Well," she said, trying to catch her breath. "From what these two told me . . ."

A realization struck Xander like a hammer between the eyes. He knew where he'd seen her before . . .

". . . mostly while running from soldiers . . ." she continued.

Xander gaped at her. If not her, then her features. The shape of her eyes. The top lip thin, the bottom one fuller. He saw them every day, staring back at him from the mirror.

" . . . I guess I'm your grandmother."

Xander blinked. His mouth formed words, but nothing came out. He shot his eyes to his brother, who had rocked back to sit on his heels.

David smiled, nodded.

"But . . ." Xander said. "How?"

"Bob," she said. "That silly cartoon face—Henry, your grandfather, made up when *he* was a kid. You put it on the tent, right?"

"But our grandpa's name was Hank," Toria said.

"Hank is Henry," she said, "like Jack is John."

"You . . ." Xander said. "*You* wrote the message next to it?"

"Yes, I was so—" Her smile faltered. "*Was?* Toria said his name *was* Hank."

Xander frowned with her. He said, "Our grandfather . . . he died last year."

"Oh . . ." She turned her head away. Her shoulders rose and fell. "I suppose . . . I mean, it has been so long. I always thought of him the way he was the last time I saw him—young. I guess all along he was marching toward that date we all have to keep."

She spoke the way Dad did sometimes. Xander had always liked it, describing things in ways he hadn't thought of before. Songwriters were masters at it, poets too. *Marching toward that date we all have to keep*—death. It made it seem less terrible. A little.

"I'm sorry," Xander said.

"And I'm sorry for you," she said. "I knew him for only ten years. You must have known him longer."

"I was fourteen when he . . . kept his date," Xander said. It wasn't quite right, but she knew his meaning. "I'm fifteen now."

"Fifteen," she said, shaking her head. "And you?" She looked at David.

"Twelve."

"I'm nine," Toria chimed.

"My goodness," she said. "I really have missed so much." Worry etched lines in her brow. "Your father, my son, is . . . is he all right?"

"Grandma called him Eddie," David said to Xander, tickled.

She touched David's knee. "Not Grandma. Call me Nana. I always wanted to be Nana."

"Yeah," Xander said. He was thrilled to give her good news. "Dad's really all right. Aunt Beth too. She's married, and you have another grandkid. Her name's Anne. She's thirteen."

"She's a grouch," Toria said.

"Toria!" Xander said.

The woman—*Nana*—smiled. "Let's see," she said.

"Alexander, David, Victoria, Anne. All royal names. My children kept the tradition. I don't suppose your mother has such a name?"

"Everyone calls her G," David said.

"G?"

All three of the King children said, "Definitely not a Gertrude!" and laughed.

"I see. And how is she?"

"She's . . . over there," Xander said, waving his hand at the portal door.

"What?" Nana said. "Looking for *me*?"

"No, she was kidnapped," David said. "Like you were."

"From this house?" Her hand covered her mouth, and her eyes welled up. "Oh . . . oh . . . I'm sorry. My dear children." She rose and hugged Xander's head. She turned to David and gave him a squeeze, then opened her arms to Toria, who came off the bench to be comforted.

As if to herself, Nana said, "This house, this awful house."

CHAPTER

forty-three

WEDNESDAY, 4:41 P.M.

David heard Dad's comfortingly familiar voice call from the hallway.

"Hello? Kids, I'm home!"

He knew his brother and sister's wide eyes matched his own.

"Dad!" he said. He scrambled out of the antechamber. He ran to Dad at the beginning of the hall and jumped into his arms. He squeezed, as if trying to meld their bodies together.

Toria and Xander collided into Dad, their arms binding them all together.

"I missed you, Daddy," Toria said. "I was so scared."

"I knew you'd be fine," Dad said. "But from what Jesse told me on the way over, you guys haven't been bored."

Disentangling themselves, the King kids spoke all at once:

"This big man chased us . . ."

"I was putting up a camera when . . ."

"Toria went over . . . I didn't know what to do . . ."

"Hold on, hold on," Dad said. "I want to hear it all, but I—" His words hit a brick wall.

David followed his gaze to Nana, who had stepped out of the antechamber.

Dad's face flashed from puzzlement to shock to joy. He backed away from this last emotion to settle on hopefulness. "Mom?"

"Eddie," she said. "You're not the little boy I've carried around in my head for thirty years. But I see him in there. I would recognize you anywhere."

Dad began walking toward her. She met him halfway, opening her arms.

"Mom," he said. They embraced, and Dad buried his face in her shoulder. He was big, compared to her. His arms seemed to engulf her.

David imagined that the last time they'd hugged, their physical proportions had been reversed, the difference in sizes even more pronounced. She would not have changed much, but Dad had been seven.

The kids smiled at one another. Toria teared up. Xander's rising and falling chest said he, too, was on the brink of losing it. David was doing a pretty good job of holding it in.

Finally Dad lifted his head and backed away a step. He sniffed and ran his palm over his face. He grinned at the kids. His eyes scanned his mother's face, studying every feature. He said, "I've missed you so much."

Her hand caressed his cheek, then she slipped her fingers into his hair, brushing it back—exactly the way he did with his children.

David marveled at this: the little things from your parents you keep with you your whole life. He wondered what mannerisms he had picked up from Mom and Dad. And that they, in turn, had picked up from *their* parents. How far back could it go, these traits?

He looked at Xander. He and his brother had the same shaped eyes. Xander's were blue, like their father's and, he knew now, like his nana's. David's were hazel—brownish green, sometimes appearing one color, then the other—like Mom's.

Xander leaned close to him. He whispered, "But it *wasn't* Mom who left the note. We *didn't* find her."

David nodded sadly. "Back to square one," he said.

They approached Dad and Nana at the center of the hall.

"Guys," Dad said. "I'm going to take your grandmother downstairs. Get her something to drink." He raised his eyebrows at her. "Something to eat?"

"Oh, no," she said. "I might need to lie down somewhere, though. I'm a bit . . . no, a *lot* exhausted. I feel so drained. Too much emotion."

Toria hopped up. "She can use my bed!" She walked up to the older woman and took her hand. "I'll get it ready for you, Nana."

Nana smiled at Xander and David. "I want to hear all about you two. We have so much to catch up on, don't we?"

They nodded.

"And we'll have plenty of time to do it, I'm sure."

David gave her a hug. Xander did the same.

"Thank you," she said. "Thank you for finding me, for bringing me *home*."

Dad escorted her down the hallway toward the landing. Toria strolled on her other side, holding her hand.

Nana looked around at the crooked hallway, at the wall sconces and old-fashioned decorations. "It hasn't changed at all," she said. She spotted something on the wall, sending her fingers to her lips.

David moved farther into the hallway to see that she was looking at four parallel furrows in the wallpaper. He and

Xander had discovered them when they'd first found the hallway.

She started weeping again, and David realized what they were: her scratch marks, put there when she was kidnapped.

They heard a sound behind them and looked back to see Keal appear on the landing with Jesse's wheelchair. He looked surprised to see another person up there with them, but he simply nodded and disappeared back down the stairs. A moment later he reappeared with Jesse and eased him into the chair.

"Jesse, Keal," Dad said. "This is my mother."

Jesse's eyes went wide. His jaw dropped open. "Kimberly?" he said.

Her head tilted. "Have we met?"

"I'm Henry's uncle, ma'am," Jesse said.

She stared at him. Slowly, she released Toria's hand and touched his. "It's been a long time, Jesse."

CHAPTER

forty-four

Wednesday, 5:00 p.m.

Keal, David, and Xander stood around Jesse's wheelchair in the third-floor hallway. The light from the strange lamps hanging on the walls flickered, flamelike. To David, it made the curving corridor appear to pulse, as if it were feeling the beating of a distant heart.

"Nana's the one who left the message on the tent," he said, hanging his head. "Not Mom."

"I see," Jesse said. "I'm sorry, son. We'll keep looking." He touched David's arm. "Look on the bright side."

"Dad's got *his* mom back?" David said.

"Well, that too . . . but I was thinking about your mother. Since your grandmother survived for so long, there's no reason to think your mom couldn't do the same."

"For thirty years?" David said. He couldn't even imagine that many years, let alone that many years looking for Mom. He'd be forty-two in thirty years.

"For however long it takes," said Jesse. "But I don't think it'll take that long. You've been looking for your mom only a few days, and you found *somebody*. That's a pretty good record." He looked around the hallway, then reached up and smoothed back his hair.

"The wind's not blowing now," David said. "Like it did last night. That was weird."

Jesse nodded. "I have to say, it's a bit frightening being up here, so close to the portals. If I'm up here and Time decides it wants me, I'm not sure I could do anything about it. Remind me to head back downstairs in an hour."

"Why does it want you in the first place?" Xander said.

"There's a balance to everything in the world," Jesse said. "Things need to be where they belong. We don't belong in the past, but if we go back there enough times, or stay long enough, history sort of . . . gets used to us. It starts to *want* us there, because by our continued presence, we made a place for ourselves. Like if you lie on a bed long enough, you get up and the mattress contains a perfect shape of your body."

"You were in this house nearly fifty years," Xander said. "Going through the portals all that time?"

"In and out," Jesse agreed. "Not every day, but a few times a week. It was enough. The past wants me back. That's why I live half a continent away. Just in case its reach is farther than I've imagined."

"Have you felt it where you live?" Xander said.

"Nope," Jesse said. "Either it can't reach that far or it forgot about me."

David looked around the hallway, at all the closed doors, at the wall lights with their carved figures of tigers and fighters and faces. He said, "You talk about it like it's alive."

"In a way, it is," Jesse said. "But in the manner in which a tree is alive. If you hack into it, sap covers the gouge and eventually heals itself. Trees adjust to circumstances, over time leaning toward the sun, for example." He shook his head. "Not alive as a human is alive, as a human is intelligent. Time abides by certain rules, the way the ocean does. A man drowns in the ocean, and we say the ocean took him. Do we mean that it consciously sought out the man and took him away? No. Time is like that: rules, but no reason."

He looked between David and Xander. "Now, while we're

up here, while I can be here, tell me everything you know about these rooms—what you call antechambers—and the portals. Everything you've seen in every world you've visited. That will tell me the best way to help you."

CHAPTER

forty-five

WEDNESDAY, 5:37 P.M.

David had just peered into an antechamber and shut the door when Dad stepped into the hallway.

"Nana's going to take a nap in Toria's room," he said, smiling. "That is, if Toria lets her. Your sister's talking up a storm." He took in the activity in the hallway—David, Xander, and even Keal moving from door to door, checking the items behind each. "What's going on?"

"Ed," Jessie said, beckoning from his wheelchair at the far

end of the hall. "When we spoke on the way home from the jail, you didn't tell me about . . . what did you call it, Xander?"

"Peaceful world," Xander said. "You know, Dad. The place you and I went, where we sat by the river and you carved Bob into the tree."

"The only world that's not violent," Dad said. He patted David's back as he headed for Jesse. "Do you know it, Jesse? You want to go there?"

Jesse's eyes closed slowly. "I know it, Ed, but no. I don't ever want to see it again."

Dad stopped. "I don't understand."

"I know." Jesse's eyes opened as slowly as they'd closed. "But you need to. You need to see it for what it is."

"What it is?" Dad said, spreading his hands. "It's one of the nicest places I've ever been. Even the air has a special quality, like . . . I don't know . . . fresh, invigorating. Right, Xander?"

Xander nodded, but his face was tight, concerned. He looked through the door he had just opened, then shut it. He moved slowly to the next door, prompting David to carry on with the search as well. But David could tell that his brother's ears and eyes were still on Jesse and Dad.

"Jesse," Dad said. He squatted down in front of the old man. "What is this about?"

"That world is not what you think it is," Jesse said. "Something terrible happened. I believe it has to do with the man who wants your house."

"Taksidian?"

"Yes, but when I knew him, he went by another name," Jesse said. "I was here when he arrived. Almost immediately, he began breaking in, going through the portals. It was then that history started changing in ways I had never seen before. Terrible, horrendous ways. I don't know why he did it, but he did."

"Hey . . ." Keal said. "You said a picnic basket, parasol, blanket, and funny hat, right?"

"That's it," Xander said.

"Wait," Jesse said, but Keal and Xander had already stepped into the little room.

Dad said, "I've been there, Jesse. There's nothing—"

"You haven't gone over the hill, have you?" Jesse said. "The biggest hill, a few miles from the lush valley?"

"No, but . . . What's over the hill?"

"The reason this house called you back."

"This house *called* me? I came back to find my mother. I—" Dad looked over his shoulder.

David saw frustration and confusion on his face.

Dad swung his attention back to Jesse. "What does it have to do with Taksidian?"

"It's the reason he's here, as well," Jesse said. "The culmination of his work. Look—" His brows pinched in concentration. "So much to tell you," he said, "and I've never been good at putting my thoughts in the best order. Age has made it worse."

"Just tell me what's over there that's got you spooked," Dad said.

David glanced into the antechamber as he walked past. Xander was setting the floppy golf cap—the tam-o'-shanter—on Keal's head.

David drew up next to his father and Jesse. He leaned against the wall, absently rubbing his cast.

"The future," Jesse said.

"But we've never found a future world," Dad said. He waved his arm around, indicating the doors. "They all lead to times in the past."

"Except that one," Jesse said. "It's why you haven't found any other future worlds. It's—"

Xander's yells came from the antechamber: "Keal! No, wait!"

A door slammed. Xander came out of the room so fast he crashed into the wall on the opposite side of the hallway. "He went through!" he said. "Keal opened the door, then he just *went through!*"

"Go get him!" Jesse said, wide eyes on Dad. "Please . . . he doesn't know what he's doing."

Dad sprang up. He rushed to the antechamber and looked in. His head swiveled toward Jesse, then David, then Xander—unsure what to do.

"Dad, I think he *fell,*" Xander said.

"Go get him," Jesse pleaded, wheeling himself forward.

"Bring him back. I'll explain later."

Dad nodded. He went into the antechamber, and Xander joined him.

David slipped past Jesse and stepped into the tiny room. Dad had the picnic basket and blanket slung over his shoulders. He picked up a butterfly net. He turned toward the closed portal door and stood staring at it, as if he hoped Keal would burst back through. He reached for the handle.

"Wait," Jesse said from his chair in the doorway. "Take this." He reached under a knitted blanket that covered his lap. His hand returned with a pistol.

"Whoa," David said.

"Jesse!" Dad said. "Where did that come from?"

"A friend overnighted it to me," Jesse said. He held it out.

"I don't want it," Dad said.

"Give it to Keal," Jesse said. "He used to be an Army Ranger."

Dad shook his head.

"You may need it," Jesse said. "I hope not, but . . . *please.*"

Dad stepped across the room, hesitated, and took the gun. He said, "You have a lot of explaining to do."

"Bring Keal back," Jesse said, "and I'll tell you everything."

Dad returned to the door and opened it. Hazy daylight flooded the little room. The fragrance of grasses and wildflowers wafted in. A warm breeze. Through the portal, a blurry vision of a meadow drifted by.

"I don't see him," Dad said.

"The portal's moving," Jesse said. "Hurry."

Dad stepped into the light. He dropped away and disappeared.

Xander reached out as if to stop him. He said, "Why the gun, Jesse?"

Jesse turned wide, almost buggy eyes on him. He said nothing.

Xander spun and leaped through the portal.

"Xander—!" David said. He threw a glance at Jesse, who read his expression perfectly.

"Don't even think it about it, son," Jesse said. "They'll be right back."

David grabbed the edge of the door as it closed. "Dad! Xander!"

Wind blew his words back into his face. The door kept closing, pushing his sneakered feet along the hardwood floor. They protested with stuttering squeaks.

"Let it shut," Jesse said.

The door shoved David into the frame. He couldn't hold it open. Pain radiated through his broken arm, spreading into his shoulders. His other arm, his legs, ached under the strain. He was sure that if he pulled away from it now, the door would catch a foot or arm and snap it off, as it had broken the baseball bat days ago. He tucked himself tight and let the door knock him through the portal like a pinball's flipper whacking a steel marble.

CHAPTER

forty-six

David fell into a patch of flowers. He rolled through them into tall grass and stopped. The air was warm and smelled like the perfume counter at the department store in Pasadena. He stared at a sky the color of a knife blade. Pollen, kicked up from his fall, floated past. He rolled over and got to his feet.

Thirty feet down a gently sloping hill, Xander rose from

the grass. He gave David a stunned look, then turned to Dad, who was a little farther down the hill, beside Keal.

Dad spotted his sons. "What are you doing?" he said. Panic strained his voice.

"I—" Xander said. He swung back to David, as if for an answer. When David said nothing, Xander said, "I want to help."

Dad grabbed Keal's arm and started up the hill. He pointed with the butterfly net. "Then catch that thing," he said. "Stop it from disappearing!"

David turned to see what Dad was pointing at: the portal. It shimmered like a heat wave, showing nothing but the door that had slammed shut behind him. As he watched, it broke apart and scattered like dandelion fluff.

"Too late," David said weakly.

"Great," Dad said. "The portal home could be anywhere." He cast a hard eye on Keal. "What's the deal? Why'd you go through?"

"I was just looking," Keal said. "I guess I stuck my head in too far. This . . . *wind* pulled me in."

"Here," Dad said. He handed Keal the gun. "Jesse said you know how to use it."

Keal took it and held it up. "A .357 Colt Python." He flipped his wrist, opening the cylinder. "Loaded." He removed a bullet, saw the curious expression on David's face, and said, "I always keep the hammer on an empty chamber.

Safer that way." He dropped the bullet into a shirt pocket. He snapped the cylinder back into place.

Dad squinted at their surroundings. The slope they were on descended a long way before leveling off. Sunlight glimmered on a river down in the valley. To their left and right, trees formed dense woods.

"You think we need it?" Dad said.

Keal shrugged and pushed the weapon into his pants at the small of his back. "Man, I don't know anything about this place, but if Jesse thinks we do, I'm glad to have it."

"All right," Dad said. "Come on." He started walking.

"Where to?" David said, hurrying to reach them.

Dad pointed at a far-off hill, past a swath of woods and several smaller hillocks. "Whatever Jesse's anxious about is over that hill. We have to find the portal home anyway, so we might as well start over there." He looked at David and Xander, giving them a tight smile. "Stay close," he said. "Give a holler if you hear or see anything dangerous."

"Don't worry," David said, "we will."

CHAPTER

forty-seven

WEDNESDAY, 5:59 P.M.

Toria sat cross-legged at the foot of the bed, facing her grandmother, who sat propped with her back against the headboard. Between them was a collection of stuffed animals.

"And this one," Toria said, picking up a bear wearing a stars-and-stripes shirt and holding an American flag on a stick, "sings 'The Star Spangled Banner.'" She wrinkled her nose. "Off-key. It's pretty bad."

She tilted her head, studying Nana's face. She pushed the bear into her lap. Softly, she said, "I'm sorry. You must be very tired."

Nana blinked slowly. "I am, but I'm also very interested in *you*. You remind me so much of my little girl."

Toria giggled. "You mean Aunt Beth. I never thought of her as a little girl, but I guess she was . . . once."

"She was only four when I last saw her." Nana smiled at the memory.

"How can you *take* it?" Toria said. "Being back after so long. I think I would just . . . *explode*."

Nana looked around the room. "Honey, after a while, you learn to adjust quickly, going from world to world."

Toria sat up straight. "World to world? You mean you . . . *bounced around*?"

Nana nodded. "But now I'm home. In a way, it's just another world for me to adjust to. But it's the only world I *want* to be in. It's the only place where *you* are, and everybody else I love."

Toria smiled. "You're supposed to be here."

"It's where I belong," Nana agreed.

Toria squinted at her grandmother's hair. A few strands were standing up, like what happens when you rub a balloon on your head and static electricity builds up. Except the hair standing up on Nana's head was also whipping back and forth.

Toria crawled over an array of stuffed animals and smoothed the hair down. "You're very pretty," she said, leaning back.

"Thank you," Nana said. "You are too. Does your mom have brown hair too, like you children?"

"Her hair's more blonde," Toria said. "She calls it dishwater blonde, but I think that sounds gross. Who'd want dishwater-colored hair? She has pretty hair, cut like this." She snagged her hair at the neckline and bent it in.

"Sounds lovely," Nana said. "I'll bet you—" She stopped. Her eyebrows came together, and she looked upward.

Toria stared at the strange thing going on at the top of Nana's head. Her hair—not a few strands, but most of it—was standing up and swishing back and forth, as though she was nodding her head underwater.

CHAPTER forty-eight

David, Xander, Dad, and Keal crunched through a beautiful forest of big trees—oaks or elms, David thought, but he didn't know much about trees.

"I can see the end, just ahead," Dad said. "We're almost at the hill Jesse mentioned."

"What's there?" David said.

"Beats me, Dae. Something scary, according to Jesse."

"Then why are we heading for it?"

"We have to know what it is. Just a peek, then we'll get out of here, okay?"

David frowned. "I guess."

"Hey, Keal," Xander said. "If you need someone to help carry that gun . . ."

"I'm fine, Xander," Keal said. "But thanks."

"Dad," Xander said, "in *The Shawshank Redemption,* these big bad guys kicked Tim Robbins's butt. You run into any of that?"

"Shawshank was a prison," Dad said. "I was in jail. There's a difference."

"So . . . *little* bad guys?" Xander said.

"No bad guys, except for the ones who locked me up." Dad stepped past the last tree and into bright sunlight, where he paused. The picnic basket hung from his shoulder by a strap. He pushed it behind him and swung absently at the grass with the butterfly net.

David stopped beside him. He said, "Sorry about coming through after you and Xander."

"Truth be told," Dad said, "I'm glad you're here. At least as long as we don't have to use that gun." He ran his fingers through David's hair and draped his hand over his shoulder.

"How'd Jesse get you out?"

"I wasn't there when he was talking to the police, but I heard some shouting."

Keal came tromping out of the woods. He carried the

folded parasol under his arm like a British lord expecting some weather. He turned his face up to the sun and held it there.

"Are we safe?" David said to his father. "They're not going to evict us or try to grab us again, are they?"

"For now we're okay, Dae. Apparently a few people in power overreacted to unsubstantiated allegations."

"Xander said Taksidian bribed people to get us out of the house and you arrested."

"Yeah, I think so," Dad said.

"So you still have your job?"

"As far as I know."

"Does that mean we have to go back to school?"

Dad laughed and mussed David's hair. "'Fraid so. Hey, Xander! What's taking you so long?"

"Watering a tree," Xander yelled from the woods. "Be right there."

Dad turned around and looked up the tall hill. The climb seemed about a mile.

"It's so beautiful," David said. "And quiet. What can be so terrible out here?"

"That's what we're going to find out."

"I hope nothing," David said. "I hope Jesse was wrong."

"I wouldn't bet against the man," Keal said.

Xander jogged out from the shadow of the trees. He said, "My back teeth were floating."

"Okay, then," Dad said. "Let's go."

David showed Xander a lopsided grin. He said, "This is serious. Couldn't you have said something more . . . gung ho?"

Xander slapped David on the back. In a deep voice he said, "It's an honor to die at your side."

"Uh . . ."

"Not what you had in mind? How about—" Smiling, Xander raised his arm as if holding a sword. "Strong and courageous!"

"That's better," David said. "Strong and courageous!"

CHAPTER forty-nine

Wednesday, 6:08 p.m.

Jesse kept an eye on the portal door from the hallway. He kept the wheelchair's footrest just inside the antechamber to prevent the outer door from closing. After all these years, being here in the house he had built with his father and brother felt somehow *comfortable.* Not pleasing, but comfortable, the way a surgeon must feel in an operating room. Or even a soldier on the battlefield. It was a place he knew well.

Here, and only here, his skills perfectly matched the challenges presented. As he had told the King children about themselves last night—prematurely, he'd realized later—he was *meant* to be here.

The lights in the hallway flickered. Jesse looked at the nearest wall light. It depicted a frowning sun face—a grinning quarter moon was poking its sharply pointed head into the sun's cheek. Light from the bulb behind the faces shone through the eyes and slits in the sun rays; it splashed up the wall to the ceiling. The light blinked out and returned a second later. The other lamps in the hall did the same.

The walls around him creaked, groaned.

Too soon, Jesse thought.

He'd been sure Time would have allowed him to stay longer before it came to claim him.

A door near the end of the hall, several down from his, crashed open. Light radiated out of the antechamber. He knew it emanated from an open portal.

He wheeled the chair back, turned, and shot down the hall toward the landing.

No wind yet. Coming soon.

Should he try to write a note? No time. Besides, sending the Kings into that world had been his most important task. A peaceful world? *Ha!*

Don't get worked up, old man, he told himself. *Not over that.*

He had shined a light on *that* dark charade.

You want to get worked up? Look behind you! Look at the portal, hungry to eat you!

He reached the landing and propelled himself out of the chair. He began crawling, moving quickly down the stairs. He tried to ignore the pain in his stomach and hips as he bounded down each step. He slowed . . . stopped.

Why no wind?

Didn't it know that if it wanted him, it had to come get him? He wasn't about to just waltz right into the portal of his own free will. He may be old, but he wasn't stupid.

A scream reached him: coming from the second floor, just below him. Beyond the collapsed walls.

Toria!

She was screaming over and over, as loud and insistent as a fire alarm.

It dawned on him.

Not me, he thought. *Nana. Kimberly. It's coming for her.*

She'd been lost in history for thirty years, thirty constant years. Of course Time thought she belonged back there.

He thumped down the remaining steps and dragged himself up onto the fallen walls. He pulled his body over the dust and debris.

Toria's screams continued.

"Nana!" the little girl yelled. "No, no, nooooo!"

Jesse reached the main hallway and turned the corner.

Banging, banging punctuated Toria's screams like a pounding drum, trying to keep time with a manic trumpeter.

"I'm coming, girl!" Jesse yelled, but the words were no more than air coming out of his lungs. He had spent his breath on moving from the third floor to the second.

"No! Nana!"

Jesse reached the grand staircase and crawled past. Toria's room was the next one on the right. He was almost there.

He could hear Kimberly now, crying, groaning with effort. Not screaming, no—all of her energy was invested in fighting the pull.

Inside the bedroom, something crashed. Toria screamed again.

His arms were tiring. He reached out, hooked his fingers on the door frame, and pulled himself forward.

Something inside the room screeched like an angry hawk. A bare foot shot out of the bedroom and struck his face. He pulled his head back. Kimberly's feet kicked the floor in front of him. She gripped the bed's footboard, her body stretched from it to the door.

That *screech!* again, and he saw the bed tremble and scrape closer to the door. Kimberly's feet came farther into the hall. They smacked Jesse's face and shoulder. He rolled away, across the hall. He couldn't help her if he was knocked unconscious.

He pulled himself slightly past the door, then arced

around, edging toward her at a less dangerous angle. "Hold on!" he said.

Toria knelt beside the bed, holding on to Nana's arms. She was crying, pulling in great gulps of air and screaming them out. Her face glistened with tears.

"Jesse! Help her!" Toria yelled. "Make it stop!"

Jesse grabbed Kimberly's feet and tried to push them back into the room.

The bed screeched across the floor. It slammed into the open door and stopped.

Kimberly's legs snapped away from Jesse. They bent around the edge of the door frame, toward the smaller hallway and the stairs leading to the third floor. They shook and twisted as though someone were tugging on them.

Jesse threw his arms around her thighs and squeezed. He heard a *crack!* Another. He prayed it wasn't Kimberly's bones giving out under the intense pressure pulling at her.

Crack! Crack!—and the footboard broke apart.

The woman shot out of the room, banged against the door frame, and turned toward the short hallway. Her body bumped over Jesse's head and kept moving. She was completely out of the room now and sliding along the floor on her stomach.

He lunged for her, seizing first one wrist, then the other. She stared at Jesse, her eyes huge and wet. Her hair whipped around like fire in a strong wind.

She said, "I don't want to go back!"

"I got you," he said.

She continued to slide, and Jesse went with her.

Toria bounded out of her room and jumped over him. She flopped on top of her grandmother, hugging her from behind.

"Toria, let go!" Jesse yelled. "Toria! If she goes, you'll go with her!"

Kimberly's eyes grew even wider. "No!" she said. "Toria, get off! Let me go!"

"I won't!" the little girl screamed. "I won't!"

They slid closer to the railing that overlooked the foyer. Jesse thought he could grab a spindle—that might work . . . for a while. As they passed, he released her right wrist and reached for the banister.

His left shoulder flared in white-hot pain. A muscular hand was squeezing his shoulder. He could not see them, but he knew long nails had pierced his flesh. Blood soaked the material of his shirt.

He gritted his teeth, telling his hand to keep its grip on Kimberly's wrist. But the pain was too great and the wind too strong.

She broke free and sailed away, sliding on the floor, taking Toria with her.

"Toria, let go!" Jesse yelled.

Kimberly and Toria reached the end of the hallway and zipped around the corner. He heard their progression toward the portal: thumping over the fallen walls; *bam-bam-bamming* up the stairs.

Toria screamed, then Jesse heard no more.

He grabbed the hand on his shoulder. It was hard as a statue's. The knuckles, the veins, the thick welt of scar tissue.

He rolled over, and the hand pulled away.

A man stood beside him, engulfed by shadows; Jesse saw only long, unruly hair, the hem of a black slicker. A soft patter, like raindrops, drew Jesse's eyes to the floor beside him. A small pool of blood grew bigger as drops fell from the man's fingers. The man leaned closer, and his thin, muscular face dipped into the light.

Jesse's heart clattered against his breastbone. He wheezed in a breath. He said, "*Dagan!* I should have known."

"They call me Taksidian now, old man." His voice was hard and dry, like bones rattling together. He looked up the hall in one direction, then back the other way.

Jesse saw the linen closet door standing open.

The man he had known as Dagan sighed. He said, "You should have stayed away, Jesse."

He reached down with both hands, and Jesse's world went black.

CHAPTER

"Wait up," David said.

Dad stopped to rest twenty yards from the top of the big hill. He turned around and scanned the valley below them. "God's country," he said.

David glanced over his shoulder. Tall green grass flowed like waves down to the woods they had traversed. A meadow of yellow and purple flowers fanned out from the other side of the trees, like glitter. A hill similar to the one on which they stood rose up on the other side of the meadow, forming a vista worthy of a postcard. The valley sloped to the river far below.

Dad pointed in that direction. "That's where Xander and I threw rocks into the river. And those trees on the other side of the meadow? That's where I carved Bob."

Xander reached David. He put a hand on David's shoulder and leaned over, breathing hard. He said, "It's steeper than it looks."

"You're more of a wimp than you look," David said.

Xander shoved him. David stumbled back and plopped down. He hopped up and scurried toward his brother, intent on sending him rolling down the hill.

"Boys," Dad said. "Not now."

Keal stepped up to them. "Whew," he said, stretching his limbs.

Dad turned and started climbing. David raced to catch up. Behind him, Xander groaned.

David reached the top first. He felt his eyes stretch wide. Dad rose up behind him and gasped.

They stood on the ridge of a hill that immediately plunged into another vast valley. Directly below them, piled up against the hill and stretching out from it for half a mile, were chunks and slabs of broken concrete. They ranged in size from small boulders to pieces that could have once been the sides of whole office buildings. Rebar jutted from the edges like severed arteries. Scattered among the concrete were clumps of metal. David recognized a demolished car and a nearly flattened dumpster. Tires were strewn everywhere. Except for an absence of paper trash, it looked like a thousand-acre dump.

Deeper into the valley, the debris assumed familiar shapes: a roadway, a bridge, the square top of a building. All of it flowed toward a centerpiece of destruction in the distance . . . the remnants of a great city. The skeletal frames of broken skyscrapers rose up from collapsed ruins, like the popsicle-stick buildings David used to make and then demolish. Smaller buildings dotted the surrounding land like an angry rash.

Vegetation had staked a new claim on the valley. Forests of trees and lush bushes streamed like water through the streets and boulevards, tall grass covered sidewalks and plazas, moss and vines climbed the buildings. It sapped all color but its own from the landscape: everything was shaded in hues of green.

And black, David realized. Many of the remaining structures were charred. The only exceptions were a smattering of elevated freeway sections that glistened white in the sun like the bones of long-dead animals.

Beyond it all, a gray mist did not quite mask an endless body of water: an ocean or sea.

Keal reached the ridge and collapsed onto his knees.

Xander rose up and brought his hand to his mouth. After a long while, he said, "Dad . . . it's Los Angeles."

David's heart skipped a beat.

Dad nodded slowly.

"I don't understand," David said. But he could see that Xander was right. He could see what was left of the U.S. Bank Tower. And the Capitol Records Building. Half of it, anyway. He'd spent his whole life in this valley, traveled its streets, attended its schools, played with children who'd once lived there. It was like standing at the casket of a dear friend.

"We did this, Dae," Dad said. "Mankind. We wiped ourselves out."

"But . . ." David couldn't get his head around it. "When?"

"Sometime in the future," Dad said. "That's what Jesse was trying to tell me. We've never found a portal that leads to the future because *there is no future*. Just this one."

"No future," Xander repeated numbly.

"Do you think the whole world's like this?" David said. "Gone like this?"

"Has to be," Xander said. "Else they'd have rebuilt it, wouldn't they? Wouldn't they have rebuilt the city, Dad?"

"I don't know, Xander."

A sound drew their attention to Keal. His face was buried in his hands. His shoulders rose and fell.

"What do you think happened?" David asked.

"War, probably," Dad said. "By the look of the buildings."

"But when?" David said again. *The future* wasn't enough of an answer.

"Jesse said it's the culmination of Taksidian's work," Dad said. "So I guess during his lifetime."

"That soon?" David whispered.

They stood, letting the seconds become minutes.

Keal sniffed. He wiped his face and got to his feet. "Ain't right," he said.

"Isn't there anything we can do?" David said. His voice had taken on a raspy tone. His throat and mouth felt dry as dust.

Dad put his arm around David's shoulder. "I don't know, Dae."

Xander picked up a rock. Grunting in anger or frustration, he hurled it out over the descending hillside. It dropped into the trash dump, clattering between concrete and metal. Just as the sound of the rock stopped, a howl rose up from the valley, close.

David said, "What was—"

A mournful wail bellowed from somewhere else.

"Hey," Keal said. "Something's moving down there."

Xander stepped forward to look. "An animal." He didn't sound so sure.

More noises kicked up: howls, screams, yips. Something clanged.

Keal's hand went to the gun in his waistband.

At first it looked to David like the shadows were shifting.

Then, from a broken concrete pipe, crawled a creature. It was fish-belly white with bone-thin arms and legs. A large head on a spindly neck, flanked by narrow shoulders. A pelt of shaggy hair clung to its skull. It rose and stood erect.

"Is that . . . a *man*?" David said.

More of the humanlike creatures emerged from the rubble. They crawled and stepped and scurried out of the shadows like individual nightmares conjured too soon. They were pale, hunched over, jittery. But—yes, they were people. Two of them bumped into each other and began fighting. They bit and scratched and rolled out of sight.

"They see us," Keal said.

Faces were turning up to stare at them. A few of them pointed. Several howled and screeched.

They began scurrying up the hill. A handful at first, then dozens and more.

"There's gotta be a hundred," Xander said.

David backed away. "Dad?"

Dad turned in a circle. He looked back the way they'd come, then toward the approaching horde.

Xander started down the hill, heading for the spot where the portal had dropped them into this world. He stopped. "What are you waiting for?" he called. "Let's go!"

"Dad," David said. "We gotta find the portal. Now." The expression on his father's face made him ask, "What?"

Dad looked at Keal. The man held the pistol in one hand.

With the other, he balanced the tam-o'-shanter on his fingers, carefully watching it as though expecting the hat to hop off his hand and scamper away.

Dad said, "You feel it too?"

"Like a magnet," Keal said.

"What?" David said. "Come on, let's go."

The first of the attacking future-humans were more than halfway up the hill. David could see their crazy, bulging eyes and the sparse, broken teeth in their gaping mouths.

Dad frowned. He said. "The portal—"

"Yes!" David yelled. "You know where it is?"

He nodded, and David knew. Even before he noticed the picnic basket quivering and lifting off of Dad's hip, showing the way home, he knew.

Dad pointed at the mob running up the hill at them.

He said, "It's down there."

NOT THE END . . .

WITH SPECIAL THANKS TO . . .

SLADE PEARCE, for *being* David: you rock!

NICHOLAS and LUKE FALLENTINE (again): you guys are great

BEN and MATTHEW FORD, insightful readers and my new friends

ANTHONY, my son and most fervent fan

JOEL GOTLER, my wonderful agent

The rest of my family, for letting me be a kid again

LB NORTON, JUDY GITENSTEIN, and AMANDA BOSTIC, editors extraordinaire

The terrific team at Nelson: ALLEN, JOCELYN, JENNIFER, KATIE, MARK, LISA, BECKY . . .

And my readers, for letting the King family live!

Reading Group Guide

1. Marguerite, the little girl David saved in the French village, grew up to become instrumental in the eradication of small pox. His heroism saved millions of people from contracting the disease. Do you believe that the things we do—whether good or bad—have a domino or ripple effect on many others?
2. Can you think of something you've done that had a direct effect on people beyond the ones with whom you had direct contact?
3. Confused by events and needing advice, Xander drives the family car to the jail to see Dad, even though he doesn't have a driver's license. Do you think it's ever okay to break rules—even laws? If so, was this one of those times? What should Xander have done?
4. Continuing his aggressive efforts to rescue Mom, Xander is willing to send Toria to the Civil War. David thinks she's too young and should not be put in such danger. In such a situation, would you have been more like Xander or David? Why?
5. David says the family needs help, and he's willing to trust Jesse to get it. At first, Xander doesn't trust Jesse. Does trusting people come easy to you? Has there been a time when you trusted someone when you shouldn't have? What happened?
6. There are many theories about time travel affecting the past. Some say it can't happen because then the people who went back in time should never have known about a world without the change (for example, they would have grown up with the change already affecting them). What do you think of the whole concept of time travel? Can you think of reasons that it should not be possible? (Don't think too hard about this one. I did once and my head exploded.)

For more reading group guide questions, be sure to check out www.DreamhouseKings.com

About the Author

Robert Liparulo has received rave reviews for both his adult novels (*Comes a Horseman, Germ, Deadfall,* and *Deadlock*) and the best-selling Dreamhouse Kings series for young adults. He lives in Colorado with his wife and their four children.